BEASTS AND MEN

BEASTS & MEN

Stories by

CURTIS SMITH

Press 53
Winston-Salem

Press 53, LLC
PO Box 30314
Winston-Salem, NC 27130

First Edition

Cover design by Kevin Morgan Watson

Cover art, "Collecting the Wild III" Copyright © 2012
by Suzanne Stryk, used by permission of the artist.

Printed on acid-free paper
ISBN 978-1-935708-75-9

for Michele, again

The light which puts out our eyes is darkness to us.

—Henry David Thoreau, *Walden*

Acknowledgments

The author wishes to thank the editors of the following publications where theses stories first appeared:

Anemone Sidecar, "The Dress"
Artifice, "The Physics of Memory and Death"
Corium, "Drive"
Fast Forward, "Belief," "The Storm"
Frigg, "No One Owns This Moment But You," "The Beach House," "The Pact," "The Cabin"
The Florida Review, "The Wolf"
Gargoyle, "Silent"
Hobart, "Movie"
The Los Angeles Review, "The Quarry," "The Hunter"
Matter, "The Dogs, the Dogs" (Shorter version)
Monkeybicycle, "Lenin!"
New World Writing, "The Nest"
Night Train, "The Diorama"
Parting Gifts, "The Couple and Their Secrets"
Pear Noir! "The Lake"
Prime Number Magazine, "The Plate Spinner"
Quick Fiction, "The Train"
Smashcake, "The Adulterers"
Smokelong Quarterly, "One Truth," "The Tycoon," "The Runner"
Stripped, an Anthology of Anonymous Fiction, "Beasts and Men"
Thumbnail Magazine, "Desert Morning, 1952"
Wigleaf, "The Twins"

BEASTS & MEN

THE DIORAMA

A mother and her son paused before the polar bear diorama. Inside, a cub huddled against its mother. A seal carcass lay before them, blood on the snow. The boy stood close. None of it was real, the mother said, a statement neither truth nor lie. The scene radiated its eerie beauty, and in the glass, her son's reflection. Perhaps taxidermy was an art form, but so was opera, and she didn't care for that either.

They passed the mountain lions. The zebras. The hyenas. Light spilled from each scene, checkerboard splashes in the dim hallway. The mother sat on a bench in the hallway's center. Her boy toured the room. He was curious but not overwhelmed. He paused before the grazing impala. The mother wondered how the impala had died, whether it had been shot or poisoned—its hide harvested for this incomplete resurrection. Her son studied the leopard latched onto a wildebeest's humped shoulder. His mother watched him, a shadow drifting through a frozen sea.

As a girl, she'd come here with her father. Certain elements struck her with unanticipated clarity. The leopard's bared fangs. The parallel and bloody wounds clawed into the wildebeest's hide. Two years ago, her father had died, and now the woman was saddened that his image had turned so slippery. She closed her eyes—searching, searching—until she recalled how small her hand had felt in his. Until she heard the soft click of his shoes. Until she smelled the rain and cigarettes on his coat.

The mother rose and walked to her son. He'd stopped before a display closed for renovations. A curtain hung behind the glass. The boy positioned himself at the glass's edge and peered through an unguarded sliver. His mother knelt beside him. Inside a man sat on a stool, his back to them. The man worked a threaded needle through a tiger's neck. The boy glanced up and smiled.

"Pretty cool, huh?" the mother whispered, as if they were trespassers, thieves of a treasure no vault or king could hold.

The Quarry

The young man plummets through the darkness. He crosses his ankles and cups his crotch. He closes his eyes, his world reduced to whistling air, the throb of his pulse. The shock of water striking his bare feet rides through him. Knees, hip, spine—every bony part registers the impact, a sharing of pain and exhilaration. He knifes downward, the quarry water cooler by the inch. Gravity yields to buoyancy. He opens his eyes into a different darkness. With a fluttering kick, he follows the path of bubbles. He breaks the surface and sucks in the honeysuckled air. He swims to the cliff's sheer rock and latches onto a scar cut by men long dead.

A woman's voice: "You OK?" Her words echo off the stone walls.

"I'm good," he answers.

He gazes up. A shadowed form falls from the stars. She is his brother's girl. She doesn't know about the letters that come from halfway around the world and their boastful stories of army nurses and local girls. The young man loves his brother's girl with a devotion silent and strong. The girl nears him. How appropriate, her framing amidst the quarry's backdrop, a space

3

mysterious and beautiful and dark, its depths littered with secrets.

She hits the water, a plumb symmetry, her feet pressed together, her long hair trailing above her head. A plume rises, and the droplets rain over the young man. The stirred current pushes against his belly. For a moment, his only company is the splash's echo, the rippling surface, the mute stars. He understands a submerged object has only two options—to sink and disappear or to rise to the surface.

THE RUNNER

Before the accident, he was a runner, a state champion in high school, a conference medalist his first year at State. On a humid Virginia night, he smashed his motorcycle into the statue of a Civil War hero. He ran again, but never like before, never again like that.

His girlfriend was a dancer. In their apartment, he asked her to dance for him. When she moved, he desired nothing, his soul at rest. Watching her, he recalled how the track had glided beneath his feet and the ecstasy of release when he hit the final straightaway. And he remembered the moment before he crashed and the night's thick scent of peach blossoms.

THE PHYSICS OF MEMORY AND DEATH

Sara wakes after midnight. The moon is bright, the room lit in indigo and bone. The lacy curtains billow. On the breeze, the scent of salt, the waves' ceaseless crash. Sara's shoulders are sore to the touch. She smells of lotion. She lights a cigarette and, with lips pressed to the window screen, blows a smoky plume. Her parents had fought earlier—too much bourbon and too many cigarettes. Now another sound, a rhythm like the surf. Soft moans. Sara rises from her bed and lays a hand on the thin wall.

A conch shell rests atop the dresser. Sara lifts the shell from its wooden stand. The shell's shape reminds her of her brother's old football. She runs a finger along the bony ridges, wipes dust from the opening's shellac-glistening tongue. Using two hands, she raises the shell to her ear.

Of course Sara does not hear the ocean. The low-frequency hiss is born from the fact that the shell acts as a closed-pipe resonator. Its wave-mimicking song is white noise, the blank slate upon which all recognizable sounds are etched. In a bit of Mobius logic, its gentle purr is also the washed-out resultant of all sounds, a tone which gravitates more than any other toward purity and which also contains almost every audible frequency.

* * *

Hot the next day, the air thick with haze and a fishy odor. Sara lies in the umbrella's shade but soon grows restless. She is annoyed by the stink. Annoyed by the radio station the boys beside them play. She tries to focus on the sounds of waves and gulls, on the call of children's voices. From behind her sunglasses, she considers her parents. There are all coping with memories, with silences and empty spaces. She goes for a walk. The seagulls hover, the shoreline thick with their calls and the too-close beating of their wings. There are no swimmers in the water, the surf overtaken by wave-nudged jellyfish, dozens, maybe hundreds of them. In the wet sand, a boy pokes one with a stick. The texture and thoughtless cruelty of the scene make Sara ill.

She lies back on her towel. Sand bristles the nook of her upper thigh. She pulls the elastic aside and brushes out the granules. Turning, she catches the boys with the horrible music looking her way. The boys smirk. One leans over and whispers into a friend's ear. Sara rises and shakes out her towel, ensuring the boys are hit in the fallout. She repositions the towel on the other side of her parents and lets the sun beat upon her face.

Friction is the rub of this world. Friction wears on a body from without and within. The smoothest surfaces are rough at the microscopic level, imperfect despite their machined polish. *Mu* is the measure of the coefficient of friction. The higher the *mu*, the greater the frictional force. *Mu* is equal to the force applied divided by the force perpendicular. Both forces are measured in Newtons, which, upon calculation, cancel, leaving *mu* as that rare phenomenon of physics, a number unclaimed by a unit's measure.

Last year, Sara's science teacher introduced her class to *mu* in a lab involving sliding blocks. Calculating the frictional coefficient was simple enough, but despite her teacher's words and diagrams, Sara struggled with the notion of *mu*. She found its lack of a proper unit vexing, the unshackled numbers threatening to flutter off like a summer butterfly, but today, on the sun-baked beach, she feels a previously unappreciated force all around her—in her mother's crinkling page turns, in the boys' music and banter, in the breeze that stinks of rot and death. Here, perhaps, lies the crux of her consciousness, the most telling confirmation she exists registered in the rub between herself and the world.

That night, they go to the boardwalk funhouse. There is always a hitch at times like these, the memory of her brother, dead these eight months. A car accident, a night of bad decisions. Gone. The funhouse would be his kind of thing. Spooky, silly, stupid. Sara is not the type to scream—yet she does, her hands clutching her father's arm when a knife-wielding woman bursts through a curtain.

They enter a room of mirrors. A dozen reflections surround her, fragmented views, distortions fat and thin. Sara grows disoriented. She reaches for her father, but she is fooled, her hand grasping air. "Daddy?" she calls.

In physics, images are divided into the real and the virtual. A real image's rays converge at a focal point, which in turn can be observed on a screen or sheet of paper. A virtual image does not exist in these terms; rather, it is a trick of the eye and the properties of light, the plaything of magicians and the subterfuge-filled origin of the phrase "done with mirrors."

Upon exiting the funhouse, Sara thinks again of her brother. Recently she's been distressed by his fading image, another abandonment, leaving her nothing more than memories and photographs, images both real and not.

Sara sits atop the sloping shoreline. The late-day sun strikes her back, her shadow stabbing far into the foaming surf. Nearby, a little boy dips a bucket into the lapping waves and empties the water over his sister's feet. A bigger wave rolls in. The boy tumbles but the girl pulls him from the water. The children yell and laugh. Seagulls hover on the breeze. The lifeguards are gone, and most of the day's crowd has left. The light is warm and yellow and rich.

A complex wave is formed by two frequencies separated by more than 7Hz. The world is awash in dissonance, two waves that mesh in an unpleasing manner. But if the resultant sound is pleasant, consonance is achieved and a chord is formed. Cultural and experiential influences surely affect the judgment of consonance and dissonance. The symphonies of John Cage and other avant-garde composers raise the question of whether our values of consonance can be altered by experience. Traditional music of the Far East, with its pentatonic scales and lack of quantitative rhythms, often registers as odd, even unpleasant, to the Western ear. Thus, unlike most of the hard-set rules of physics, the values of consonance and dissonance appear to be flexible and open to interpretation.

Sara listens to the children. What a deceptively simple magic, their voices able take the surf's crumble, the caw of gulls, and elevate them into chords. Sara closes her eyes. She hears her brother's voice and hers, arguing, laughing, teasing. An echo. A chord. A song she will carry in the cage of her bones.

THE ADULTERERS

The adulterers struck the golden retriever on their way to the motel. The dog sprang from the roadside. A blur, a muffled thump. The man pulled over. "That was a dog, right?"

She looked back. The brake lights shone red, then darkness. "I think."

The man retrieved a flashlight from the backseat. He told the woman to stay behind, but she didn't. Neither bothered with their coats, and by the time they reached the dog, they were shivering. The man switched on the flashlight. The dog lay broken before them. Steam rose from the gash that stretched from midsection to tail. The breeze rippled its fur. Sprinkles of down tumbled across the gravel.

The adulterers crouched. The woman placed a hand on the dog's side. The man shone a light into the beast's dull eyes. A car passed. The man and woman squinted in the headlights' sweep. The woman hooked a finger beneath the collar. "Think we should call?"

The man stood and brushed off his pants. "No."

Back in the car, the woman cried. Her son had a dog he loved so much.

DRIVE

Hang up the phone. The governor will not issue another stay. A dry-air drowning seizes your lungs. Two hours until midnight, and suddenly, your house, a space in which you've felt lost and adrift since your wife's death, strikes you as claustrophobic.

Walk through the hushed June night. Smell the flowers and mulch, the scents a reminder that your garden is thick with weeds. The dark soothing, but even this dulled world chokes you with its familiarity. You anticipate the houses of neighbors. The sycamores' peeling bark. The playground where your son once cried atop the jungle gym, too frightened to climb down.

Stand on the sidewalk outside your house. The streetlight angles toward your door, shadows across the lawn. Your keys jangle, but instead of going inside, you start your car. Tell yourself the full tank is an omen.

Drive. How easy, the traffic at this hour, the lazy pulse of cars beneath metered streetlights. Flow onto the interstate. Billboards and industrial parks slide by, anchors liquefied by speed and your thoughts' easy drift. An hour passes. You head north; then west on an interstate you've never traveled.

Pass the state line. Hills press upon you. Rivers appear then wind away. Check the dashboard clock. The man who murdered your son is dead now. White lines stream through your headlights' shine, the wilderness all around.

Drive. The radio off, the windows down. The night air cools your brow. You never took your son camping, despite your best intentions. Drive.

Head west, through the hills. West, until you reach the flatlands. The speedometer hovers at eighty. In your rearview, the hilltops shade red. Once you explained the earth's rotation to your son using a globe and flashlight. He spun the globe faster and faster. Continents blurred into oceans. Your gas gauge flirts with E.

Take the next exit. There's a filling station, a restaurant, a motel. Your shadow stretches before you, a thin stain over the macadam. The day will be hot, you feel it in the air. Turn back, a hand shielding your eyes. The sun has broken over the hills. Consider the dawns you've witnessed after sleepless nights and arrange them into a portrait that says more about you than words ever could.

Step into the diner. "Coffee, please," you tell the waitress, the silent hours stubborn in your throat. Your eyes and lips dry. You are a stone heavy with sleep. For years, you yearned for a stranger's death. Nature seeks balance. Consider osmosis. Consider diffusion. Consider the bell curve. Within you, the hatred has ebbed into a greater longing for your boy. Let the state have this man. Let your son be left to you.

* * *

Study those around you. The coffee warms your throat but it brings no lift. Waitresses scurry through the kitchen's swinging doors, plates and saucers balanced. At the counter, talk of gas prices and triple-digit heat. Truckers and construction crews come and go. It's a day like any other; a gift beyond price. A plate arrives, food you don't remember ordering.

Eat. Eggs, bacon, potatoes. Your fork scrapes the plate, a devouring, a refueling. The waitress smiles. "You were hungry, sweetheart." Ask her the name of this town.

Follow your shadow across the lot. In the motel lobby, the early risers, suitcases in tow. The woman at the desk says a check-in this early will cost two nights if you stay beyond noon. "That's fine," you say.

Ride the elevator. The motion tugs your stomach. The hallway stretches before you, each step begging to be your last. Your journey is near its end. Your room is small and clean. Pull the curtains, the sunlight reduced to window-hugging slivers. Turn on the TV, the volume low; you want to wake to a human voice. Undress, your clothes piled by your feet, and slip between the sheets. Through heavy eyes, study the room. Remember a motel stay years ago, your wife beside you, your boy jumping wildly on the other bed. The smile he wore that day follows you into a dreamless sleep.

SILENT

Silvia nods for yes. She points. She shrugs. If pressed, she forms the most minimum response then retreats. Silence is her shield. Her kingdom.

On her desk, a sketchpad. The paper's ripples remind Silvia of a breeze-touched pond. The texture is designed to snag charcoal flakes, but Silvia prefers her special pens. Charcoal is dull, vague. Silvia's honed pens hiss across the rough paper. Her strokes proclaim; they cleave. This morning she shades in the creases of Sean's leather jacket. At the class's front, Mr. Kuhns delivers his daily speech about positive attitudes and behavioral goals. Sean rubs his temples. Silvia and Sean and seven others occupy this basement classroom. Among the students of Wilson High, this stark setting of white walls and well-spaced desks is known not as room B-106, but simply, "the pit."

Silvia crosshatches the shadows beneath Sean's jittering boot heel. Sean's a paranoid. Leo is delusional. Kate's a cutter. The Ramsey brothers are sociopaths, and Aubrey is an early stage schizophrenic. They swallow daily doses of Clozaril, Risperdal, Paxil, Luvox, Zyprexa, Haldol, Thorazine, and a dozen more. Some mornings, when the light is at its grayest, auras born of man-made powders and twisted histories radiate from their skin. Crazy people see auras, but Silvia knows the world hinges on exceptions.

Silvia's pen scratches the paper. Mr. Kuhns pulls a chair to Sean's side. Sean abandons his temple-rubbing for strikes of his fist against his thigh. Mr. Grove, the pit's burly aide, glances up from his newspaper. Mr. Grove cracks his neck, a readying for the confrontation that may explode at any moment. Silvia perks up as well, only she is enthralled. Unlike Sean and Leo and the rest, Silvia is here by choice. Silvia stopped counting the psychiatrist's questions after sixty-seven, her defiant hush noted on every page of his report. After Silvia's recent dealings with the police and their suspicions, no one questioned the old man's findings. Silvia's pen hurries to capture Sean's hair-pulling fingers.

A voice over the intercom announces the art class field trip is to report to the cafeteria. Silvia brushes her black bangs from her eyes and gathers her pens and pad. Mr. Kuhns asks Mr. Grove to escort her upstairs. Sean slams his palm against his forehead and curses God.

Mr. Grove does not attempt to talk to Silvia. *Clomp, clomp, clomp* go his Goliath's shoes, each weighty footfall registered in Silvia's green sneakers. Silvia peeks into the classrooms along the way, the bleary first periods where teachers lecture students yet to fully wake. Silvia's hand cups the cigarettes and matches in her jacket pocket. The long hallways are deserted save a few stragglers and the other art students headed to the cafeteria. A locker slams. Silvia's faint reflection drifts across the trophy case's glass. A corner of the cafeteria has been claimed by the art class students, all with jackets and sketchpads in tow. Mr. Douglas, the art teacher, and the trip's chaperones sip coffee by the cafeteria entrance. Mr. Grove guides Silvia to an empty table behind Tania Hillman and her friends.

Tania is one of the school's popular girls, a basketball

star, tanned and blond. Her boyfriend's varsity football jacket drapes the back of her chair. The tail end of a pink cashmere scarf dangles from one of the jacket's pockets. Tania sets her phone to speaker and plays a popular song, the acoustics tinny and shrill. Tania stands to practice a dance move. Her hoofing maneuvers trigger laughter from the others at her table. Mr. Douglas watches then returns to chatting with the chaperones. Any other student would have been told to turn off the music and sit down, but Tania, through her athlete's status and her role on dance committees and student council, has earned a degree of leeway, a bit of entitlement she exploits daily with her loud hallway chatter and preschool make-out sessions, in her habit of traipsing into class in the seconds after the bell has rung.

A possessed voice echoes up the hallway. The boys near Silvia stand, and the conversation at Tania's table crumbles to a halt. Sean's arms flail as Mr. Kuhns herds him toward the office. Sean's threats and sobs rattle through the cafeteria. Mr. Grove huffs over to help corral the boy. The chaperones pull back as the trio passes. Her dance interrupted, Tania reclaims her seat. Silvia flips to a new page in her sketchbook and begins drawing the boy sitting alone at the next table. Her pen scraping, Silvia etches the boy's scruffy hair and the discolored skin surrounding his swollen-shut eye.

"What the fuck are you doing?" Tania asks.

It takes Silvia a moment to realize Tania is speaking to her. Silvia follows Tania's gaze to the place where Silvia's sneaker tip meets the slack cuff of Tania's jacket. Tania yanks the sleeve away. "Leave my shit alone, pit freak."

Tania's friends laugh. Silvia brushes the bangs from her eyes and stares at Tania. Mr. Douglas cups his hand by his mouth and announces: "Let's move out, folks!"

Tania stands and yanks her coat from the chair. "About fucking time."

* * *

Silvia claims the bus's last seat. She places her sneakers upon the space beside her and balances her sketchpad against her propped knees. The aisle's line halts behind Tania as she kicks a sophomore out of her desired spot. Michael, the boy with the black eye, sits opposite Silvia in the third seat from the back. Silvia rejoins her sketch. Last weekend, Tania's boyfriend decked Michael in the 7-11 parking lot. Silvia's overheard the rumors in art class these past two days—the flattering portrait Michael had drawn of Tania swiftly handed over to her boyfriend, the picture torn to shreds after their one-punch fight, the pieces fluttering over Michael's prone body as his attacker cursed and spat.

The bus lurches from the school lot. The museum is a half-hour ride. On the expressway, the bus picks up speed, and Silvia holds her pen tighter. The familiar backdrops of strip malls and gas stations give way to boarded-up houses and graffiti-choked walls. For every suburb, there is a ghetto. For every clique-brimming high school, there is a pit. Silvia finds comfort in this. She finishes her portrait of the boy with the black eye as the bus nears the museum.

Mr. Douglas stands. "OK, ladies and gentleman, remember our agenda." He raises his voice to be heard over the gathering of coats and pads. "From now to 11:30, you are free to wander the first two floors. Your assignment is to sketch any piece that speaks to you. We'll meet in the cafeteria for lunch at 11:45." Tania and her friends stand, ignoring the teacher's gestures to remain seated. Tania checks her jacket pockets, then ducks to glance beneath her seat. "Tania," Mr. Douglas says, "will you please—"

"My scarf," she says. "It's missing."

"I'm sure you'll find it—"

"You don't understand," Tania says. "I just had it. It's pink. Cashmere. It cost a lot of money." She addresses those around her. "Has anyone seen a pink scarf?"

By now the others are standing. Silvia brings up the end of the shuffling line. Tania, her hand wedged in the crevice between the seat and its back, studies Silvia as she passes.

Mr. Douglas has to reboard the bus to get Tania. Outside, the others shiver in the chill. Bulldozers and backhoes crawl across the field behind the museum. Swirls of parched dirt envelop the machines. Birds peck along the temporary chain-link fence surrounding the site. Mr. Douglas exits the bus and addresses the group. "OK, people, our agenda is set. Does anyone have any questions? Tania?"

"Someone has to have my scarf," she says. "I had it on the bus."

Mr. Douglas sighs. "And yes, please keep an eye out for Tania's scarf."

He leads the way up the wide, brownstone steps. The museum is classic Greek revival, Doric columns, horsemen carved into the long frieze, a crowning cornice. Silvia pauses halfway up. She blows her nose and stuffs the used tissue into her jacket pocket. A fire engine, its siren wailing, speeds past. In the near distance, a black plume rises over the rooftops and leafless trees. Silvia breathes deeply, hoping to taste a hint of burnt wood and plaster.

The museum's lobby is a grand concourse. Branching staircases lead to the upper floors, and far above, a tessellation of cloud-gray skylights. Mr. Douglas and the chaperones hand out admission pins. Silvia is sliding the pin into her jacket's lapel when Tania jostles her. The pin pierces Silvia's skin, and a tiny dollop of blood spots her fingertip. Mr. Douglas, unaware of Tania's shoving, steps between them as he doles out more pins. Tania points to her neck and mouths the words *my scarf*. Silvia's stare echoes the blank gaze of the concourse's statues. All feelings for this foul-mouthed girl flee her heart, Tania no more human than the flowers Mr. Douglas arranges in his coffee-tin vase. Silvia has stared down the girl gangs in juvie and the psych ward's crazies, and in the process, she's gotten her ass kicked more times than Tania has dry humped her boyfriend in the art lab's darkroom. Tania wilts and turns back to her friends.

Mr. Douglas reminds everyone of their time constraints then wishes them well. Her pad tucked beneath her arm, Silvia wanders to the antiquities wing. She presses a tissue against her finger's wound until the bleeding stops. Her sneakers squeak as she circles a statue of a nameless king. A hundred testaments call from their glass tombs: a Spartan's battle helmet, coins bearing Caesar's profile, a sundial from an Aztec temple. Silvia pauses before a grinning fertility statue. Encased in its lit prism, the statue seems to float in the gallery's darkened space. Silvia claims a bench, turns to a new page in her sketchbook, and clicks her fine-tipped pen.

Michael approaches her. "I think this one is cool, too." He gestures toward the bench. "Do you mind?"

Silvia scoots over. They work in silence, his charcoal whispering, her pen hissing. He leans over. "I like yours." She considers his drawing, two takes on the same piece. "You can hear me, can't you?" he asks.

She flips a back a few pages and shows him the sketch she drew on the bus. "Does my eye really look that bad?" he asks. He pulls out his iPod and offers one of the earbuds. His thumb spins the wheel. "I'm thinking Bach. How about you?"

She secures the bud into her ear. A violin plays, a piano following in time. Silvia finds the music playful and lovely and somehow perfectly harmonious in this treasure-filled room. The minutes pass. She loses herself in her work, her narrow bands of ink massing into illusions of shape and depth. She studies both her hand and Michael's, their work an echo in this room of relics, a reminder that what lasts in this world is not the flesh but the deeds of the flesh.

* * *

Silvia and Michael stand in the bustling cafeteria line. Surrounding them are old people, kids from other schools, college-types in hipster clothes. Silvia places a yogurt and a juice on her tray. Using her body to shield them from the cashier, she slips an apple into Michael's jacket pocket. The back of her hand rubs his stomach, and he returns her smile. They eat at a crowded table. Silvia accepts the earbud Michael offers. The Ramones play "Rockaway Beach," the cafeteria's din in her other ear. Mr. Douglas circulates between the tables, reminding his students they have an hour on their own after lunch before they're to meet in the lobby. Silvia chomps at the apple and examines the pulpy imprints of her teeth. In the corridor outside the cafeteria, she hands Michael her sketchpad, holds up a finger that tells him she'll just be a minute, and slips into the restroom.

She emerges from the stall and washes her hands at a sink. Suds circle the drain. She lifts her head, and in the mirror, she discovers Tania and her friends. Silvia's heart leaps until she notices the hitch in Tania's swagger, a hiccup lost on Tania's phone-and-jewelry-loving posse but glaring to an observer like Silvia. Tania blocks the way when Silvia reaches for the towel dispenser. Tania buries her hand into Silvia's pocket and pulls out her pen.

"I know you have my scarf, fucking pyro thief." Tania drops the pen. Silvia stoops to retrieve it, and as she stands, Tania digs into Silvia's other pocket. Used tissues, some spotted with blood, flutter onto Tania's ballet flats. "Fucking gross," Tania sneers.

Silvia attempts to slip past her. Tania snares her coat's sleeve. "Not so fast, bitch."

Silvia latches onto Tania's wrist, rips it away, and braces Tania's hand, palm-up, between them. The faucet drips. The fluorescent lights hum, and the scene plays out in duplicate in the long mirror. The throb of Tania's pulse rides into Silvia's fingers. With a swift jerk, Silvia raises her pen-holding hand, clicks the plunger, and slams the honed tip into the meat beneath Tania's thumb. A current connects the girls, a flow of revulsion and elation, a primal electricity amplified by the extra twist Silvia gives before yanking the pen from Tania's palm.

Tania and her friends stare at the expanding crimson puddle. Blood snakes across the lines of her palm. Silvia releases her wrist. "Fucking whore," Tania says, harsh words blanched by shock.

Silvia lunges forward, her pen held an inch from Tania's watering eye. Tania staggers back against the sink. "Don't! Please!" Tania shrieks. Silvia holds the pen for an unflinching moment before wiping the bloody tip against the jacket's varsity letter. Tania's friends shrink back when Silvia heads to the door.

In the corridor, she brushes past Michael. He calls for her, but she keeps walking, a clipped pace toward the museum's rear doors. She steps outside. The cold calms her sputtering pulse. She shakes a cigarette from her pack and places the filtered tip between her lips. A dirt-speckled breeze stirs from the field behind the temporary fence. A dump truck lumbers past. Beyond, in the museum lot, the school buses wait in a line of yellow. Silvia strikes a match and the flame warms her cupped palms. Fire engines howl in the distance.

Michael joins her. He carries her sketchpad and his. "What went on in there?"

Silvia skews her mouth and blows her smoke away from him.

"Are you OK?"

She sucks a final drag and extinguishes the tip with a twist of her sneaker. She is about to take her sketchpad when she's distracted by a fluttering commotion along the fence. The brown grass at the fence's bottom shudders as a pigeon tries to escape from a cat. The bird's gray wing beats against the chain link, its body lifting just above the grass, a crippled resurrection the cat snuffs again and again. The cat's paws flash. Feathers plume, a few stuck to the fence before they're carried off on the breeze.

Silvia runs forward. The cat scampers off and crouches in the weeds ten yards away. Silvia and Michael stand over the bird. Nestled in the trampled grass, the pigeon lies on its back. Gashes mark its heaving midsection, the down ripped aside. One wing is horribly bent, and the other flaps spasmodically. The cat rises to study the scene. Silvia kneels in the matted grass. The bird's head twitches, its eyes as black as tar. The violence of heavy machinery trembles in Silvia's body. Michael kneels beside her. The pigeon opens its beak and emits a pained call.

Silvia unzips her jacket. From an inner pocket, she produces the pink scarf. She folds the scarf, once, twice, three times, until it is barely larger than her hand. In health class, she practiced CPR chest compressions on a plastic dummy. She strikes the same pose, the scarf covering the bird's head and torso. She presses down and delivers her weight in a sharp thrust. Hidden beneath the soft material, the crunch of bones and skull. The pigeon's good wing stiffens then sags. Silvia pulls back and wipes the scarf in the grass.

Michael turns from the bird to Silvia. "Did you really burn down your parents' house?"

Silvia stands. "Come on," she says.

They jog to the parking lot. The pink scarf trails behind Silvia like a captured flag. They weave between the buses until they find theirs. The bus is locked, but Silvia, having bunched the scarf into a tight ball, manages to slide her hand between the rubber-edged doors. Michael helps by pulling back one side. She tosses the scarf, an arcing, unraveling flight that barely clears the second seat. She raises herself on her tiptoes and offers Michael a single kiss on the lips.

The class gathers in the lobby. Mr. Douglas performs a head count before leading the group outside. A statue of a Civil War hero gazes down upon them; the pigeons atop his bronze shoulders take flight as the students approach. Smoke no longer rises from the nearby rooftops, but Silvia imagines the fire's scent spread across the city, a residue embedded in the jackets and lungs of a hundred strangers. An undertone of whispers circulates until Tania's injury comes to Mr. Douglas's attention. Tania presses a wad of paper towels over her palm. The group reaches the bus and begins to board. One of the chaperones is a nurse, and pulling Tania aside, she and Mr. Douglas examine the wound. Silvia lingers near the line's end, close enough to overhear Tania tell Mr. Douglas how she hastily reached into her purse and jabbed herself with a pen. Mr. Douglas retrieves the bus's first aid kit. Before she climbs aboard, Silvia stoops and picks up one of the bloody paper towels Tania has dropped.

Silvia again claims the last seat. Michael sits directly opposite her. Through the bus's dirt-smeared window, Silvia watches the chaperone bandage Tania's hand, the gauze wrapped then secured with tape. The bus driver turns the key, and the engine rumbles. Before Tania can take her seat, one of the girls up front stands and waves the pink scarf. "Is this it, Tania?"

The girl leans over and drapes the scarf around Tania's neck. The pink material strikes a vibrant note against the bus's shadowed hues. Tania's bandaged hand lifts the scarf, and she glances toward Silvia. The bus lurches from the lot.

Silvia bunches the bloody paper towel until it resembles a crimson rose. Cliques and pits—she will never escape all her cages, yet with a lit match or the drawing of blood, she can conjure a little justice. She swings her sneakers to the floor, and Michael slides over and offers her an earbud. They sit together for the ride home. They are silent, their jostling knees touching. In their ears, music they alone share.

THE LAKE

I.

When the weather was nice, the fisherman and his girl spread a blanket over the shore's rough sand and watched the cargo ships cleave their way to the docks. The cargo ships' hulls weighed heavy with iron ore from Minnesota and pulpwood from Canada. The ships were dull-eyed and ugly. They didn't care how they looked. It wasn't important to them. The sun, warped and bloody from the city's pollution, sank into the water. The cargo ships faded to shadows then disappeared.

The fisherman and his girl built driftwood fires and sipped warm cans of Iron City. They studied the stars and the dark spaces between them. On the night they learned of her pregnancy, they returned to the lake. A storm was coming. Gusts of wind blew flat and strong against the pines. Over the lake, the thunderheads crept closer, billowing layers illuminated by the lightning they hurled into the heart of the lake. The waves chopped against the shore. With the air full of rain and electricity, it felt like creation itself.

II.

Tackle box in hand, the fisherman stepped from the shore. His breath, bitter with coffee—and as the day passed, whiskey—crystallized the moment it escaped his chapped lips. December through February, he could walk the shoreline and count the human links like himself that stretched from Buffalo to Toledo.

His boots crunched over the snowy ice, and the sun had yet to rise. Twenty winters had come and gone. Back home, his wife slept, warm beneath the covers and adrift in dreams she no longer confessed. They used to be in love, but now they shared something else, a knack for survival perhaps, but he was not certain. Their children had grown, their boy in the army, their girl a stranger. The fisherman sawed a hole into the ice. Beneath him, the walleyes paraded in sluggish rhythms. The fisherman lowered his line and waited for the invitation that would connect their world to his.

One Truth

She'd punched a boy on the bus. Square in the mouth, once, then again. Her father had to come to the elementary school to get her. In the principal's office, they watched the surveillance tape. The principal in his suit and tie, her father in his insulated coveralls and rubber boots. The girl with the nurse's ice bag on her aching hand. The video mesmerized the girl. The image, soundless, unflinching, rendered in sketchy gray, may as well have been the vision of God. Three times they watched it, the principal's pudgy fingers working the VCR's buttons. Each viewing added to the image's immutability. Still, in the girl's gut, a denial, the realization that one truth wasn't necessary all truths.

Silence on the ride home. The pickup rattled over narrow roads. The snowy fields rippled with wind-sculpted crests. Not a bird in the sky. Her father's face gaunt and wind-chapped. Back home, her father sat her at the kitchen table with her books and assignments. His only words—she was to stay put and attend to her studies until lunch. So she completed a math paper and wrote a paragraph about a butterfly's life cycle. When she was done, she set down her pencil and flexed her swollen hand. She gazed through the frosted window. Outside, her father chopped wood. She worried about the ax, the sharp blade, the cold-slick handle. He swung the ax again. The split wood tumbled. The dull thump lingered in the girl's chest.

The girl returned to her schoolwork. Word problems, friends sharing apples, how many would each get and how many would be left. The girl rubbed the eraser beneath her chin. She couldn't think of apples and make-believe friends. Outside, another thump of the ax. There was a time when her father's wood-cutting was as steady as the kitchen's ticking clock, but that was no longer the case.

Her dog lay beside the heater. The girl climbed from the chair and crouched next to the dog. Up close, a gentle hum from the heater, a circle of warmth. The dog lifted its gray muzzle, sniffed, then lowered its head. Its shaggy tail thumped the floor. She kissed his brow. "Who's a good boy?" She stroked his faded coat and thought of the hidden tumors that would take the dog before spring. She thought of life at its simplest, the mechanics of heart and lungs, the betrayal of cells.

The door swung open. The girl's muscles clenched against the cold. The dog struggled to stand, an honoring of its master. Pale red on her father's cheeks. The scent of wood smoke on his jacket. The girl returned to her seat and picked up her pencil. Her father hadn't worked since spring. The girl often caught him walking with a steadying hand laid upon walls and countertops. Sometimes she reached over and cut his food; on his face, the expression of a man contemplating a book written in a strange language. "Come with me," he said.

She grabbed her coat from the back of a kitchen chair. The coat fit snug over her sweatshirt. The cuffs rode above her wrists. On the sleeve, an oil stain from her father's garage. The boy on the bus had said he wouldn't wipe his ass with something so ratty. He was about to say more when she filled his mouth with her fist.

The girl and her father stepped outside. A porch of sagging planks, potted geraniums dead beneath their snowy caps. Her breath steamed. The yard's bare sycamore splintered the sky. They stepped into the garage. Clutter all around, naked light bulbs overhead, sawdust on the floor. In the corner, the wood-scrap desk her father had built. Two boxes waited atop the desk. He handed her one and took the other. She followed him back outside.

Ice rimmed the drive's potholes. The dog's nails clicked over the gravel. The dog trotted a few steps, slowed, then trotted a few more. Inside the girl's box, catalogues and newspaper, the rubber-banded stacks of hospital bills they could never hope to pay. The drive rose slightly. The fields her uncles farmed lay buried beneath the snow. The wind blew dry and gritty. White below, gray above. The horizon naked and blurred, a lost boundary.

The girl and her father emptied snow from the rusted barrel. He lifted his box and delivered an avalanche of paper. The girl did the same. A crumpled envelope tumbled across the snow. They stomped the boxes flat and shoved them in the barrel. Her father sprayed lighter fluid and pulled a box of matches from his pocket. She studied her father's hands, the blue veins, the nicks and scars of his machinist's trade. The fingers that had taken apart their pickup's carburetor now trembled. The motion reminded the girl of the sycamore's clattering branches.

The matchbox fell. The girl picked up the box and threw the matches that lay scattered across the snow into the barrel. "Let me," she said.

She ran the match across the striker. Sparks, a whiff of sulfur. She dropped the match into the barrel.

The flame caught. The dog staggered back on arthritic legs, its snout twitching. The flames burnt red and orange. A column of black smoke twisted toward the clouds. The girl held her hands near the barrel. The warmth felt good in her swollen knuckles. Her father rubbed her shoulder. "Lots of things aren't fair, sweetheart."

THE BEACH HOUSE

The woman rented a beach house. A week of no phones, no TV. The gulls cawed for the rising sun. The afternoon breeze tattered the shouts of her boy. At night, she laid a hand on the sun-warmed cheek of her sleeping child. The sound of his breathing folded into the crumbling surf, and here, she believed, might be the heartbeat of this earth. The house's owner arrived every day after lunch and swept the porch. He cursed the salt, the humidity, the sand. He claimed all man's creations were fated to rot, an omega poisoning every alpha.

Unable to sleep in her own bed, the woman nestled beside her son. Years later, after he'd grown into a man, the woman would remember the owner's words. And she remembered her son's colorful towel drying on the porch railing. And the cold sting of the garden hose they'd used to wash the sand from their feet.

MOVIE

The men with the chainsaws scrambled in the trees. The boy sat across the street, his bike by his side. The earth shook with each dropped limb. A few leaves clung to the branches, the limbs' insides hollowed by rot. The men on the ground fed the limbs into the chipper. The chipper whirred, the drone of a thousand bees. A brown current spat from the chipper's chute.

The tremors of the chipper and chainsaws remained with the boy as he rode off. Along the way, he passed his friends; they carried fishing poles and nets and boots. When the boy reached the old man's house, he performed a rodeo rider's dismount, the bike lying on its side, the front wheel still spinning. The curtains in the old man's house were always drawn. The light hurt the old man's eyes. The boy peered through the front door's screen. The baseball game played on the radio. "Hello?" the boy called.

The boy stepped inside. Blinding, the darkness after the afternoon's sunshine. He remained still and waited for his eyes to adjust. The first thing he noticed was the radio dial's shine in the old man's oxygen tubes. The old man's palsied fingers reached forward, and the boy accepted the five-dollar bill. Before he pulled away, the old man seized his hand. His grip's strength surprised the boy. "Thank you," the old man said.

The kitchen smelled of medicine and rotting fruit. The boy filled a water glass. The heat built as the boy followed the old man up the steps. The old man grasped the handrail, the other hand clutching the oxygen tank. The boy waited as the old man caught his breath short of the final step.

They entered a small bedroom. In the room, a chair and an 8mm projector atop a tall stool. The old man took a framed picture from the wall and rested it on the floor. The wall was blank save the rectangular patch less faded than its surroundings. The old man collapsed into the chair. He shielded his eyes. "The window," he gasped. The boy handed him the glass. The old man adjusted his oxygen tube and drank. His thick tongue licked the water from his lips.

The chainsaws' distant wail faded when the boy closed the window. He pulled the shade and drew the curtain. He turned on the projector's lamp. A lit square appeared on the wall. The vent above the bulb shone. Dust motes drifted through the vent's lit shafts.

"Nurse," the old man said.

Beneath the stool, a stack of circular tins, and on each, a strip of cloth tape. The boy shuffled through the tins—*Schoolteacher, Waitress, Secretary*—before finding *Nurse*. The boy attached the reel to the projector's raised arm. With a spin, he unwound the film, a strip of illegible squares. He opened the motor's casing. Squinting in the unshielded glare, the boy threaded the film over sprockets and rollers. A flick, and the motor caught. The film sputtered forward. The boy secured the tail to the take-up reel, shut the casing, and turned the motor off.

"Ready?" asked the boy.

The old man nodded. The boy turned the motor back on. The film loop stammered. The boy adjusted the focus.

A black-and-white image appeared, a nurse in a small office, her skin and outfit shaded by the wall's yellow. "Go," the old man said.

The boy paused before closing the door. On the wall, a close-up of the nurse's pretty face, a woman now old, perhaps dead. The old man pulled his chair forward until his shadow became part of the scene.

In the kitchen, the boy filled a water glass and took it to the porch. The late-day sun knifed through the trees. In the distance, the chainsaws revved.

THE PACT

Kate took the dog, a terrier the size of a football. Little Banquo. That was the easy part. The leash, the bowl, the dog—she could carry them all at the same time if she had to. Harder was shaking the pills into Jake's palm. They'd made a pact when this mess started. At first the pact only concerned the dog, but then it grew into something more.

She lifted the glass to his mouth. A skeleton in white sheets. Rot beneath his skin. She wiped water from his lips. In her recent dreams, he was made of ash. Ashman. She told him this because he loved words. "Ashman," he repeated. His smile a reminder of better times. She told him of Ashman's Phenomena, a type of tachycardia. "Be still my beating heart," he said. Later, she cried. In her dreams, the Ashman's fate was never easy.

So much had been taken from him. So much dictated. Pincushion veins. A diaper. His taste reduced to textures and oddly disparate flavors. Ginger. Soy sauce. The final act would be his. Mozart on the stereo. Lilies in a vase. A favorite book of poems. "I'd say a little indulgence is in order." A grin. Then another spasm, pain's muting current. Kate fluffed the pillows in the way he liked best.

The dog, of course, and the pills, too, if that's what he wanted. Anything. Anything at all.

After the final pill, he asked for the bag. His voice dry. Promises had been made. He slipped the bag over his head. She remembered him on a snowy day, a wool cap he used to wear. "Thank you," he said before the plastic eclipsed his mouth. The bag rose and fell. Its awful rustle mesmerizing. He spoke once: "I am weak. Forgive me." She assured him he was not. He reached for her hand. She listened to traffic outside his window, a rattling fan. Finally, stillness. The plastic clung to his parched lips.

She removed the bag. A dreamer's sweet expression. She touched his damp cheek. Her hand lingered until he cooled. The things she took: the dog, the leash, the bowl, the pills and bag, a cardboard box filled with his unpublished works, the bottle of expensive whiskey she'd bought him last year. "We'll drink this when you've shown this thing who's boss."

That evening, she swallowed a pill and cracked the bottle's seal. The stars above, a summer's long drought. Her yard's brown grass rustled beneath her shoes. She set the box on the patio. She squeezed the lighter fluid. The scent of fuel, a dizziness in her head. The forgotten rhythm of rain. Banquo sniffed around the wilted rhododendrons. Kate struck a match and tossed it into the box.

The papers caught. A burst, the flames higher than she'd expected. A flush for her face, a heat deeper than summer. The flames settled. His words disappeared, the neatly typed and the ones penned in his tight scrawl. In the hiss and sizzle, she heard his voice, a remembered joke about Kafka's estate. "I should be so talented," he'd said. She dropped the plastic bag into the flames. The plastic billowed. A captured glow inside, an iridescent moment then consumption.

Kate sat in a lawn chair. The whiskey bottle on her lap, her dangling fingers lost in the dog's fur. She closed her eyes and watched the afterimages of dancing sparks. She thought of the empty space she'd carved today. Heaviness in her bones, the pull of the things she'd ingested and done.

Banquo's barking rousted her. The box now engulfed by flames. She hadn't considered the cardboard, the vessel as sure to burn as its contents. Stirred by the heat, the burning pages scattered across the lawn. Kate ran for the garden hose. The papers snared in the rhododendrons' parched stalks. The flames multiplied. The light grew. Around her, a cathedral ablaze.

BELIEF

The ping pong ball bounces over the tightly packed glasses. Mesmerizing, the bony notes, the ball's erratic dance. The center's red glass earns a prize from the coveted top shelf. There must be a plausible strategy, some twist in one's release, but Aubrey has yet to grasp the connection. She hands the next child three more balls.

Aubrey watches the ball. The baby inside her kicks. She taps her stomach's curve, and the baby kicks again. It's a game she plays, a call and response that eases her loneliness.

Stringed lights hang from the rafters, electric starshine for the base's rec hall. Christmas carols play over the crackling PA. The children tumble across inflated castles. Echoes, a hundred echoes. A few larger figures wade amid the throng, parents in camos, the base commander in his dress blues. Stooping, the adults chase and tickle, a tribe of loving giants.

"Who's next?" calls Maureen, Aubrey's table partner. Reindeer antlers bob atop Maureen's head. She is nearly old enough to be Aubrey's mother. Aubrey is thankful Maureen is here, her cheer and enthusiasm making their gaming table one of the more popular stops. Earlier, when Maureen stepped outside to call her teenage children, Aubrey felt lost, her voice barely a scratch against the din.

Two corporals burst through the doors. The music stops. The sudden breeze brings the scent of the sea. The soldiers stride forward, their chests thrust. "Attention!" barks one of the soldiers, and both corporals jerk into stiff salutes. The castles' inflating motors purr, but the bouncing has stopped. The doors open again. The children gasp. Santa has arrived.

Their motors cut, the castles melt into plastic puddles. A charge fills the air, a current of hope and dreamed-of reunion. Santa makes his rounds, the dumbstruck and giddy believers by his side, the tentative in an outer orbit. The base commander and Santa exchange salutes.

Maureen slips on her coat. "Mission accomplished," she says. The noncoms are already taking down the other tables. Outside, dampness on Aubrey's skin; chilly, yes, but far from the winter cold of the place she still considers home. She gazes to the sky and thinks of her husband beneath the same stars half a world away.

"Sure," Aubrey says when Maureen suggests a ride into town. Aubrey has nothing waiting but a quiet apartment and a book she's not sure she wants to finish. Rust circles the wheel wells of Maureen's car, but the interior is clean. At the gate, she jokes with the sentry about a red-suited intruder.

A deeper darkness waits outside the razor-wire fence. The road is flat, sand on the shoulder. In the brush, orange eyes flash then disappear. Aubrey cracks her window. The salty air sinks into her lungs. Maureen says this will be the third Christmas in the last four years without her husband.

They hit town, a main drag of strip malls and super-markets, and in the older parts, churches and bars. Soldiers on every street. A boy on a bike darts in front of them. Maureen fiddles with the radio until she finds Christmas music. The reindeer antlers remain upon her head. She reaches beneath her seat and produces a pint bottle. "Do you mind?" she asks.

They drive to the suburbs, a neighborhood known for its Christmas-light displays. Here, the streets wind in gentle arcs, the houses set far back from the curb. Maureen parks along the end of a cul-de-sac. She pulls a long drink from the bottle. She's quieter now, her smile gone. A silhouette passes across a bay window.

And the displays are beautiful! Trees wrapped in white, illuminated branches reaching to the sky. Wax bags line the sidewalks, a candle burning in each. The shine against the darkness makes the houses seem weightless, like they are a breath away from breaking free of the earth and returning to their rightful place among the stars.

Maureen tips the bottle again. Aubrey smells the alcohol, harsh and biting. Her baby kicks. Maureen claims her husband is a good man but naïve. He thinks he's fighting for his country, but here, she says with a sweep of her bottle-holding hand, is who he's really fighting for.

A sip, that's all Aubrey wants, a taste to forge a comm-union with this time and this woman. The warmth floods her throat, a shudder down her spine. Before she can hand the bottle back, the police lights flood their car.

* * *

Aubrey sits on the curb, hands upon her head. The strobe's red pulse illuminates Maureen's straight-line walk. Another squad car arrives. Along the cul-de-sac, forms gather behind the windows, curtains pulled aside then shut. The officer holding the breathalyzer to Aubrey's mouth studies her belly. Aubrey squints when the light is shone into her face. Her raised arms grow heavy. She answers questions, *Yes, sir; no, sir.* She explains they just wanted to get off base and see some Christmas lights.

Maureen sits on the curb beside Aubrey. One of the officers holds the bottle, the street's beautiful lights shimmering in the glass. He threatens them with a night in jail, but instead he allows the women to return to base as long as Maureen doesn't drive. Maureen says nothing, but Aubrey thanks them, once for her and once for Maureen. She slides the seat back to accommodate her girth. The cruiser haunts the rearview until Aubrey returns to the poor part of town.

Christmas decorations hang from Main Street's light poles, candy canes and plastic trees, all of them tattered, survivors of winter storms long past. The reindeer antlers rest on the dash. Maureen lays her head against the passenger window. It's only when Aubrey turns down the radio that she realizes Maureen is crying. Aubrey wishes she knew what to say, but that part of her is empty tonight. Instead, she turns up the radio, and her voice reflexively joins the carol's chorus. It's a song she knows from childhood, a time when she went to church and believed such things.

LENIN!

In the early years of the previous decade, Connor Phelps captured the nation's heart as the hero of the surprise blockbuster *The Littlest Soldier*. Connor, sparkling and blond, breathed life into the role of Dee McElroy, a boy lost with his golden retriever in the Arkansas wilderness. The movie's first act culminated with the crash of Captain James Mitchell's rescue helicopter. Little Dee, relying on spunk and fear and a desire to save them both, shepherded the blinded pilot through a dozen tribulations until they stumbled, half-dead, upon a backwoods church. A joyous hymn called to them: "Stronger, Jesus, you are stronger than me! I cannot fight you anymore! I am yours! You are mine! I am yours!" Dee and the blind pilot staggered through the church doors, and the congregation, black and white, brothers and sisters in poverty and belief, swept them into their rapture, their voices and hands lifted to the heavens as they embraced the weary strangers.

Weeping was common during viewings of *The Littlest Soldier*. The second act's end, the death of Dee's beloved dog, Hopper, was the main offender, the scene so gutturally resonate that it earned a spoiler reputation

41

not seen since *The Crying Game*. The reviewers and intelligentsia debated—was *The Littlest Soldier* the schmaltz fest they'd all expected or were the plot's simple workings of loss and salvation a deceptive metaphor, a story so benignly straightforward that it was nearly lost on a cynical world? Connor Phelps took home a special Oscar that year. His speech, full of the plucky and awestruck notes audiences so loved from *The Littlest Soldier*, only further endeared him to the public.

For the next three years, Connor Phelps possessed first dibs on Hollywood's meatiest child parts. While he never caught fire as he had in *The Littlest Soldier*, he did accrue a string of solid money makers as the boy who played matchmaker to his widowed mother, the boy who bravely battled cancer, the boy who endured spastic humiliations before receiving his first kiss. Connor and his notoriously protective manager/mother had picked his roles carefully, but even she couldn't halt the aging process. The adorable child sprouted gangly limbs, his aw-shucks voice a pained roller coaster. Every pimple, every awkward stab at independence was magnified a thousand-fold in the gossip rags. Connor turned down the lead in the blockbuster remake of *The Goonies* to star in *The Violet Garden*, a Victorian parlor piece in which the young man's discomfort with everything from his accent to his ruffled collars was painfully etched in each frame. That disaster was followed by the outright cataclysm of Flint Bartholomew's comeback vehicle, *Captain America, Freedom's Crusader*. Connor was tapped as the Captain's trusted sidekick, but the role offered inane lines, uninspired fight scenes, and a superhero costume one critic called "the most embarrassing use of spandex since *Staying Alive*." Later that year, Connor joined the rarified pantheon of actors who'd won both an Oscar and a Razzie.

Of course there was still work, but the choicest roles were now shunted to the pretty faces recruited from the Disney Channel's prefabricated-pop offerings. Connor mailed in performances for *The Deadliest Curse* and *The Gipp, Ronald Reagan's Early Years*, but in his reunion with the director of *The Littlest Soldier*, Connor immersed himself in the underworld of white supremacist gangs to star in *God's Calling*. The film and Connor's role earned decent praise from the critics, but the public had no interest in seeing little Dee McElroy sporting a shaved head and swastika tattoos. Connor's audience appeal was now officially damaged goods, an image further tarnished with his firing from the set of *The Deadliest Curse 2* amid speculations of cocaine use and drunken carousing.

Tragedy came into his life with the death of his mother during a scuba diving excursion in the Canary Islands. The who's-who of Hollywood came to pay their respects, but Connor, toxic with tequila and pills, upstaged her funeral with a collapse his agent would spin as "emotional exhaustion." Before Connor left the hospital, he was blindsided again by pitiless fortune in the form of his mother's lawyer. Mrs. Phelps, it turned out, had made a string of dubious investments, racehorses, reservation casinos, wheat futures, and more. Connor Phelps, whose estimated wealth had once flirted with fifty million, was now down to his last hundred thousand.

A troubled and hazy period followed—dust ups with the police and paparazzi, a paternity suit, a tabloid tell-all from his mother's former assistant, a failed television pilot. At the age of twenty-two, after ramming his cherry-red Porsche into a police cruiser outside the Viper Room, Connor was sentenced to four months in supervised rehab for his second DUI and possession of unprescribed Xanax. The Daily News's front page featured a dazed Connor, his head streaked with blood and his wrists shackled. "The Littlest Junkie" proclaimed the headline.

Here, the story of Connor Phelps deviated from the self-destructive trajectory so common to the entertainment industry, for upon his release, he married one of his nurses and returned with her to her hometown of Billings, Montana. He granted no interviews, and the press, having enough scandal unfolding daily on the streets of Los Angeles, moved on to the latest fall star. Connor's wife worked in a pediatrician's office, and Connor became an adjunct then full-time theater professor at Rocky Mountain College. He directed his daughter's first-grade Christmas pageant, and in his way, became one of town's best-loved citizens, a once-famous actor who was never too busy to stop and sign an autograph in the aisles of Home Depot, a man who'd lived the glamorous life only to find contentment with real people in a city as proudly American as any other.

A week shy of his thirty-third birthday, Connor received a call from Hayden Frank, a costar from *The Deadliest Curse* and an ex-partying cohort. The two talked of old times, Connor laughing but also nervous, the thought of his former self enough to make him ill at ease with a man he once considered his friend. Connor congratulated Hayden on the success of his directorial debut, a biopic about the Rat Pack and the Vegas mob. Hayden shared more good news: the studio had given the green light to his new venture, and he asked Connor to consider returning to Hollywood to test for the lead role of Vladimir Lenin.

Connor's first response was a reflexive "No," but Hayden pressed, appealing to notions of flattery and ego long dormant in Connor's life. Connor said he'd think about it and get back to Hayden by week's end. The next day, a biography of Lenin arrived, a book thicker than any Connor had ever read. On the title page, an inscription from Hayden: *To an old friend—In this man's spirit, I see you.*

Connor read as his wife drove to Los Angeles. In his mind, an image gelled of a revolutionary who yearned to give a voice to the voiceless, the classes exploited by the heartless mechanics of industry and war. In each highway rest stop and motel, Connor considered those he met, the ones shackled to minimum wage jobs, people stooped by a lifetime of merciless labor, and his thoughts often returned to the words his friend had written—*In this man's spirit, I see you.*

Mountains, valleys, irrigated flatlands, sprawling suburbs, and finally, in a fit of concrete and glass and steel rising before the sea, Los Angeles. Connor's stomach tightened. Here, the transgressions and failures of his past proved unavoidable, and on the trendy downtown boulevards, he felt the resurrection of the ghost he'd fought to bury, the self-centered man-boy who'd bought drugs in this parking lot or screwed a groupie in that alley. By the time they reached the studio gate, Connor was grappling with the initial pangs of a panic attack, and perhaps if he had been at the wheel, he might have turned around, a rubber-burning retreat back to the anonymity of Billings. The guard checked his clipboard, then stooped to stare inside. He grinned and pushed up the bill of his cap. "Welcome back, Mr. Phelps."

Variety trumpeted Connor's landing of the role with a front-page headline: "The Soldier Returns!" Sensing a monumental miscue or the season's most sentimental comeback story, reporters crammed the preshoot press conference. Connor, sporting a Lenin-like goatee, fielded the reporters' questions with self-deprecating modesty. He told them how he'd grown to appreciate the wonders of Big Sky country, and how the love of the good woman sitting beside him had turned his life around, a confession which brought tears to both their eyes. An army of cameras captured their impromptu kiss.

They repeated the heart-tugging scene at the airport. Connor rubbed his thumb over his wife's glistening cheek and promised he would fly home whenever his schedule allowed. He stood at the security checkpoint, waving when she turned, and when she melted into the throng, he understood that a part of him was leaving, too. The process had already started, the belief that method and craft would allow him to bring his character to life, and until shooting started, he spent his days secluded in his rented bungalow, revisiting highlighted passages from the book, jotting notes, and contemplating his mirror reflection. He read and stared, stared and read, staring and reading until the man in the mirror was neither him nor Lenin but a new entity altogether, a hue as unique as the overlapping circles in a Venn diagram.

For the next three months, Connor Phelps delved into this hybrid creature. He unplugged his television and only used the computer for his nightly Skypes with his wife and daughter. He read by candlelight, shaved with a straight razor. He ate the set's catered fare, but at his bungalow, he limited his diet to black bread and boiled meat. His weight loss threw the costume designer into a tizzy. Every day, his makeup woman shaved his head, and when Connor rubbed his bony scalp, he felt focused, his life honed to him, his work, and this man who'd died long ago. The interior scenes were shot at the studio; the exterior saved for the final two weeks in the snowy Sierras. Here, the tech crews had erected ramshackle huts based on the only photo of the Siberian village to which Vladimir and his fiancée Nadya had been exiled. Nadya was played by Jamie Stevens, a young woman attempting the transition from tween TV to movies. As the winds howled and the snows piled upon the shacks' sagging roofs, Jamie and Connor retreated to rehearse in the warmth of her trailer.

Having filmed the death scene weeks ago, the last day of shooting proved anticlimactic. Still, emotions ran high, and with Hayden's final yell of "Cut!" Connor and Jamie hugged each other and crumbled into tears. The crew clapped, and Hayden joined them, squeezing them both, an embrace cut short by his ringing phone. As the crew began to break set and seek warmth, Connor listened to Hayden argue with the studio exec who was now insisting that an exclamation point be added to the title.

The Reverend Jim Underwood paid to see the first matinee of *Lenin!* in Biloxi's twenty-screen multiplex. Along the way, he'd said his hellos to the ticket seller and the young woman who'd sold him his Coke and Raisinets. As the leader of Biloxi Baptist and as president of both Christians Championing Traditional Morals and its companion cable ministry, Reverend Underwood was a well-known man in town. Names often escaped him, but he cherished the greetings of near strangers, faces he'd seen in the pews or during one of the many charity events his church sponsored.

The Reverend settled into the high-backed stadium seat. He was anticipating the movie's promised escapism, a two-hour respite from ringing phones and the financial woes that had beset his ministry. *God would find a way* had always been his belief, but the hard numbers of his debts promised little hope, and he could no longer ignore the prospect of shutting down his cable operations. He sighed. Perhaps this was for the best. He'd always lacked the showmanship and easy outrage of his television brethren. In the Bible, where so many of his fellows had found the constant threat of damnation, Reverend Underwood had discovered an elegant plea for compassion. Man's role, Reverend Underwood believed, was to honor God in one's heart and actions, but in recent years, he'd grown despondent by those who paid lip service to the Lord's message of brotherhood while wielding His name like a sword against those who viewed the world differently.

Reverend Underwood slipped the first Raisinet past his lips. He wasn't a regular movie-goer, the devoting of a whole afternoon to himself a luxury he rarely enjoyed, yet he was looking forward to this. He'd seen *The Littlest*

Soldier at least a half dozen times, most recently with his grandchildren, a viewing during which he, despite knowing what lay ahead, cried with them when Hopper died. In *The Littlest Soldier*, Reverend Underwood divined deep parallels to his own mission—a child, made strong by innocence and belief, leading a blind man from the wilderness. The Reverend had also enjoyed Phelps' other roles, and during the days of the young man's personal struggles, the Reverend had prayed for him, seeing in him an echo of many others he had counseled through darkness and doubt. Every so often, Reverend Underwood would come across a mention of Connor Phelps, the "Where Are They Now?" features that showed side-by-side photos of the The Littlest Soldier and the man he had become. Reverend Underwood smiled at the images, happy that the young man had found happiness far from the hollow, earthly dreams of Hollywood.

So it was with great interest that Reverend Underwood first read of Phelps' comeback in *Lenin!* Surely Phelps would portray the revolutionary with sympathy and insight, but also with the truth that a misguided man could be Satan's tool. The Reverend planned to base a sermon on the film, the decay of the Soviet empire a metaphor for the emptiness and heartache waiting in a life without God. In his most private thoughts, the Reverend imagined writing Phelps a letter; in return, the actor would visit his studio, an interview they'd start as strangers and end as friends. Maybe even kindred souls.

The house lights dimmed. At first, Underwood was taken aback by Phelps' resemblance to Lenin; yet in his blue eyes, Underwood also detected the boy from *The Littlest Soldier.* The camera followed Lenin's muddy boots as they marched down a squalid street, the focus racking back to take in the whole of a wretched village, a panorama of brutality and poverty and filth that reminded Underwood of his missionary work so many years ago. On screen, a woman died of hunger. A wealthy man whipped his carriage driver. Underwood sat forward, moved in a way he hadn't expected.

But as the movie neared the hour mark, Underwood began to feel betrayed. True, the camerawork was hypnotizing. The crisp dialogue allowed Phelps to bring a primal solidness to his role, but the movie's overt romanticism appalled the Reverend. Gauzy close-ups and love-story undertones glossed over the real history surrounding this man. The Reverend had paid to see a movie of a man-turned-monster, and while he hadn't expected blood, they at least could have shown his teeth. Gathering his coat and empty soda cup, Reverend Underwood left as the final credits rolled.

Upon returning home, he took a long walk through his neighborhood. He studied the backyard play sets abandoned in the early January chill, the dormant gardens, the Christmas decorations waiting to be taken down. The financial woes of his ministry faded beneath this peaceful scene. He thought of the good people he knew in this town, their freedoms and their faith. As a man of God, he had witnessed his share of suffering, both here and abroad, and he, more than most, appreciated the gift of his country.

Back in his study, he put the sermon he'd been working on in a drawer and pulled out a blank page. He wrote not about Connor Phelps or Hollywood but about the dangers of foisting one's hopes upon an unsuspecting soul. How unfair it was, both to ourselves and those we projected upon, and to illustrate his point, the Reverend offered the story of himself and Connor Phelps. Perhaps, he suggested, his listeners would be better off buying a DVD of *The Littlest Soldier* than seeing *Lenin!*

Neither in the pulpit nor on air did Reverend Underwood mention boycott, but it didn't take long for his most strident followers to adopt the word as their rallying cry. The bloggers, already keen to swoop upon the movie, posted their takes, many citing the nonexistent boycott declared by Christians Championing Traditional Morals. The bloggers' cries spread, a wildfire swiftly parroted on conservative talk radio. The argument conveniently shed Reverend Underwood's theme of misplaced hope and focused instead on intellectual elitism, the movie cited as the latest salvo in the culture wars the left had been waging for decades against the American soul.

The first organized protests met Thursday moviegoers in Galveston, Tallahassee, Montgomery, and a dozen other cities. Fights erupted as ticket holders and protestors confronted one another, the fisticuffs and arrests broadcast worldwide in near-real time on the Internet. On Friday, prints of *Lenin!* were stolen from projection booths in Roanoke and Oklahoma City, the latter burned in the parking lot, the fire cheered by the placard-waving mob. In Nashville, a teen protestor was hospitalized after he fell from the marquee he was attempting to chain himself to.

That Saturday morning, Reverend Underwood returned to his study. Before him, a new sermon, an appeal for civility. His wife tended to the phone that had been ringing for the past four days, requests for interviews from newspaper and TV reporters. The Reverend rubbed his temples and wondered how his words had gotten so twisted.

A knock came from the study door. His wife stepped inside. She wore an apron over her housedress, her hair pulled into a gray bun. In her hands, a pile of opened envelopes. "It's the mail, Jim."

He sighed. "Yes?"

She laid the envelopes before him. "There's over fifty-thousand dollars in donations." She locked him in a hug so tight it stole his breath. "It's a miracle, Jim!"

Tor Enberg strummed his acoustic guitar. The TV played, the muted news channel, videos of sports highlights and floods and men carrying guns in the street. Snow fell outside his apartment window, the Norwegian winter of gray and white. On the coffee table crowded with empty beer bottles and ashtrays lay the textbook for his morning class. A senior at the local university, Tor had spent the morning contemplating his future as a mathematics instructor, a prospect he today found as gloomy as the weather and his hangover.

He strummed again, realigning the chords he'd been wrestling with all morning. For the past two years, he'd played in a band with some college friends. They performed covers, blues and rock mainly. They practiced like the students they were; the band run like another study group, each member expected to share and speak. Sometimes they were lost, apes making angry noises; other times, they wandered into a jam's timeless bubble. Here, they exchanged smiles, elated to have found one another in the single-hearted manner understood only by children and musicians and lovers. Emboldened by last semester's rowdy gigs at the town's best bars and coffeehouses, they'd discussed cutting a demo CD, but the project had yet to transcend conjecture and daydreams.

Sometimes Tor convinced the others to sneak in the handful of his originals they fiddled with during practice. During these tunes, the audience often appeared politely lost, searching for a memory they'd never owned, their smiles returning only after the band launched into the next familiar cover. Tor played his chords again and frowned at the result. Playing other people's songs had been fine at first, but this morning, Tor viewed these tunes as little more than dead ends, stale clichés in a world already drowning in banality.

He continued to strum. On TV, images of protesters, their faces snarled, fists shaking. Next, a snippet from *The Littlest Soldier.* Tor recalled the last time he'd seen the movie, he and his hash-smoking band mates mocking the plot's saccharine tone but all of them wet-eyed by the end. Another shot, this one of the boy's grown-up incarnation as Lenin huddled in a rattling boxcar. Finally, a grandfatherly preacher high in his pulpit. Tor smiled. How typically American, the manufacturing of self-righteous drama.

Tor kept playing. He thought out loud, words strung into a joking tale about Lenin stepping out of that boxcar and into the modern world. The notion made Tor grin, and he returned to his story, the second verse seeing poor Vladimir lost in a mall, the aisles of the Gap as daunting as the jungle, his skeptical heart finally won over by a Big Mac. Tor turned to a clean page in his math notebook, and as he scribbled, a chorus welled within him, a complement as easy as two jigsaw pieces fitting together. A rush of creativity seized him. He missed his first morning class then another, breakfast and lunch forsaken until he finally fell asleep on the couch, the guitar clutched to his chest.

Tor shared the song with his band at their next practice. Tor strummed and sang, running through the tune twice, the lyrics interrupted to suggest the others' parts. On the third go-round, Olaf added the bass and introduced a playful link to the bridge. Christian fashioned a staccato guitar hook. Erik provided the backbeat and teased a trilling cadence from his hi-hat. Their first tries proved ragged, but soon they'd molded their sounds into a catchy whole. When they were done, they sat for a moment, smiling, the last notes fading before they burst into laughter.

Tor named the song "Poor, Poor Vladimir." He and his band played the tune all that winter, often two or three times a night, the audiences singing along with the chorus: "Vladimir, Vladimir, it's all right. Vladimir, Vladimir, let's dance tonight!" At those moments, when the room rollicked with the voices of many raised as one, all of them singing *his* song, Tor's heart swelled. They cut a demo with a handful of other originals. The University station then the local radio put the song into rotation. Tor's plummeting grades were offset by the upswing in his personal life, the interview requests from the local media, the manager who now handled their schedule, the beautiful girlfriend who danced seductively by the stage during their gigs. Tor was on his way to take his final exam when their manager called. Sony had offered them a record deal.

Finance Minister Valentin Sidrov contemplated the reports lining his desk. Money. It always came down to money, all the theories of economics he'd learned at the University less pertinent than the shell games con men played on city streets, a sleight of hand that stole here and hid there, always hoping not to get caught. Valentin attempted to arrange the reports from the most pressing to the ones he could set aside for the time being, but the task only further depressed him. There were crumbling bridges and leaking pipelines, dilapidated sewage plants and electric grids pushed to their limits. Valentin rubbed his temples, imagining his desk as a map of Russia and each report as a brush fire, the country he loved tangled in a cycle of neglect and crisis.

He pushed himself away and began to pace. The high ceilings of his Kremlin office did little to ease his sense of suffocation. The portraits of men who'd previously occupied this grand space stared back at him, their stern faces lit by the chandelier's warm shine. Valentin paused by the painting of a predecessor rumored to have been poisoned by Stalin in this very room. Valentin grinned; perhaps poison was preferable to the report he would be forced to give later today.

A ding announced an incoming email from Valentin's son. *Check this out*, the note read; below it, an Internet link. Valentin clicked and found himself watching a YouTube clip. The video began with a scene from *Lenin!*, the *Littlest Soldier* actor shivering in a boxcar, the steam of his breath pluming before his face. The movie was a huge hit, even though certain scenes were rumored to have been altered for the Russian release. Valentin had thought the movie satisfactory, a bit glossy, obviously the work of a non-Russian but still engaging despite its broad strokes.

In the video, Lenin closed his weary eyes. The scene faded, and from the darkness came a song's drumbeat intro. Of course Valentin had heard the Lenin song. Who could have avoided it this past month? The tune had worn on him, but he couldn't deny its infectiousness. He'd seen the band's video, a bunch of long-haired young men, three looking like children at play, one oddly serious for such a lighthearted song, but the image now on Valentin's screen was an amateur shot of nightclub dancers gyrating and shaking their hips in an oddly synchronized performance. Once the chorus hit, the images switched back and forth between the dancers as they pounded their chests and raised their fists and a scene from *Lenin!* where the Littlest Soldier performed the same motions as he rallied workers in the Saint Petersburg shipyard. The video then cut to another packed nightclub, this one labeled as Munich, where the dancers performed the same moves. Other scenes followed—young people from clubs in London, Bombay, Singapore, Kobe, Mexico City, Rio, Johannesburg, and more.

Valentin recalled his own flat-footed attempts at the Hustle during the oppressive days of Soviet fear. He smiled at the ways of the young, their whims and fads, his own son's fascination with his computer and phone. How important it had once been to Valentin, an admitted ideologue more comfortable with a book than a young woman, to own a pair of Levis and dance in an underground discotheque.

He turned off the computer and donned his coat and hat. Perhaps a dose of fresh air would clear his thoughts. He strolled into Red Square, the spring day bright but cool. The walls of the Kremlin rose behind him. Saint Basil's painted domes reached toward the blue sky. Sunlight glinted off golden crosses. Pigeons scattered at Valentin's approach, his shoes clicking over the bricks. In the stones beneath his feet, he felt the echoes of tanks rushing to meet Hitler's Panzers, the cries of dissidents butchered by Ivan the Terrible, and Valentin, knowing history, also understood there were no answers to be found to his problems. All he could do was squeeze a pittance in one spot and pray his actions wouldn't lead to an even greater suffering in another. He walked past those waiting to enter Lenin's granite mausoleum. Older people mainly, some carrying red flowers, but in the mix, younger ones, too. Years had passed since Valentin had visited, but with a flash of his credentials, he was allowed to the line's front.

It took Valentin's eyes a moment to adjust to the mausoleum's dim light. Grim sentries stood at the ready, rifles in hand. The visitors filed past. Whispers only, a woman attempting to stifle her cough, the men with their hats in their hands. Photographs and smoking were prohibited. Valentin fell in line behind a waddling woman and a young man in a leather coat. Lenin lay in his glass tomb, a pose of sleep, yet comfort denied by his suit and tie. How small he looked, the body dwarfed by its opulent surroundings.

Outside, Valentin donned his hat. The old woman and young man in the leather coat paused in front of him. The young man held out his phone, and the woman laughed at the dancing video Valentin had seen earlier. The man and woman walked off, their shoulders touching as they watched the clip. Valentin remained behind, struck by a notion so audacious that he needed a moment to fully grasp it. He walked, then ran, the architecture of centuries and czars long gone blurring past. By the time he reached his office, he was sweaty and out of breath.

His secretary stood. "Is everything OK?"

"Yes, yes." He rushed past her, and she followed him into his office.

"Your meeting with the President is in an hour."

He opened his computer and began to type. "I know."

The initial Lenin's-body tour was slated for the former satellite countries of Eastern Europe. Valentin, having grudgingly won over the President and his cabinet, had envisioned these engagements as a testing of the waters, a position from which an honorable and unheralded retreat could be executed.

Valentin paced the cavernous rotunda before the Warsaw opening. He supervised the placement of metal detectors and the shelf arrangements in the adjoining gift shop. A worker dusted the newly made stand of polished wood, a scaled-back replica of the mausoleum's magnificent altar. Valentin glanced out the window. A modest line had formed. A street vendor sold red flowers and miniature Soviet flags. The museum workers studied Valentin, awaiting the order to place the glass coffin atop the pedestal.

Dmitri Benko had accompanied Valentin. A thin-shouldered, dour man, Dmitri was the official mortician of the Lenin Mausoleum, the grandson of the undertaker who'd embalmed the fallen leader. Dmitri, with his silences and chemical smells, unnerved Valentin. The prospect of traveling with him through Europe was not a welcome one, but Valentin soon learned he could ignore the morbid little man for he seldom spoke, preferring the company of the corpse over Valentin and his entourage.

Valentin knocked then opened the door off the rotunda. "Dmitri?" he called.

Dmitri did not answer, his focus intent on the syringe he had slid beneath the corpse's collar. Earlier, he had provided Valentin with his itinerary—the daily rounds of makeup and injections, the spot cleanings and the lint rollers he ran over the suit—and then the weekly bath, a sight Valentin hoped he would never witness.

Dmitri withdrew the syringe, its tip covered by a cloth so as not to spill a drop. He spoke, his gaze fixed upon the corpse. "We are ready."

Under Dmitri's supervision, the museum workers placed the glass coffin atop its pedestal. A perimeter of gold stanchions and velvet ropes circled the shrine, the space occupied by two hulking guards. The waiting crowd had grown, the line stretching beyond the corner. Valentin checked his watch and nodded to the curator. The doors opened.

The two-week stint in Warsaw exceeded Valentin's greatest expectations. The gift shop sold every item the first day, and Valentin phoned in rush orders, the offerings extended to mugs, playing cards, T-shirts, peasant caps, and snow globes. A ritual developed—each day at noon, young and old would gather outside the museum and dance to "Poor, Poor Vladimir." The crowds grew daily, and by the second week, the police were forced to block off the street for five minutes to accommodate the boogieing mobs.

The frenzy intensified in Sofia, and by the time they reached Bucharest, Valentin was busy arranging a swing through Europe's capitalist heart. Fiat won the bidding war to serve as the tour's official backer. The IMAX version of *Lenin!* accompanied the exhibit, the audience in their 3-D glasses reaching out to touch a ghost. The protestors and scuffles only ensured greater visibility. Each day, the museum custodians swept away the small mountains of mementos and flowers and hand-written notes. In Paris, over two thousand crammed the Louvre courtyard in hopes of breaking a Guinness Record for the largest massed dance. The Kremlin website added a Lenin Gift Shop link, but its server crashed beneath the onslaught. When *Lenin!* led the Oscar nominations, Valentin accepted Coca-Cola's offer to sponsor the North American tour.

High in the private jet carrying the exhibit from London to its Los Angeles opening, Valentin studied the Atlantic, the cloud shadows and horizon-stretching ripples. He sipped cognac, savoring the warmth in his throat. He comforted himself with the belief the tour had achieved success beyond the financial, the history of his homeland now experienced by many, the corpse a testament to his people's struggles and faith. His gregariousness fueled by his second cognac, Valentin sent word to have Dmitri join him for a drink, but the little man declined, preferring to keep vigil by his charge in the plane's cold storage area.

The cordoned-off block outside the L.A. museum hummed with activity. Reporters and camera crews jockeyed for favorable backgrounds. Ticketholders lined the sidewalk. Vendors weaved through the throng, their T-shirts offered to everyone except the police and the crazed protestors penned behind zebra-striped barricades. Valentin and Reverend Underwood bumped shoulders in the middle of the street, each offering an apology before they moved on, their focus distracted by the breeze-rippling, three-story tapestry draping the museum's sun-catching east face. On the tapestry, a portrait of Lenin, one hand on his lapel, the other raised and clutching a Coke. Beneath, the brand's latest slogan: *Start your own revolution!* Valentin showed the guards his security clearance and stepped inside the museum. Underwood ducked beneath the barricade, wary of the palpable anger which had infected his followers.

Connor Phelps dressed in a Beverly Hills hotel room. Jamie Stevens, his *Lenin!* co-star, lay sleeping in the bed, the sheets tangled around her naked body. Connor had jetted out a few days earlier, his week jammed with interviews and appearances. He'd hoped for a private viewing of the Lenin exhibit, a solemn conclave with this man he'd tried so hard to understand, but his manager had persuaded him to attend the public opening for maximum exposure. Connor's head ached—champagne had never agreed with him—and he was surprised to find a second empty bottle of Dom in the bathroom. His cell rang, a call from his waiting limo. Connor hunted through the room's mess for his belongings. In his blazer's vest pocket, he discovered a folded note. *Good luck Daddy!* He shoved the note back into his pocket and opened the door. "Who's there?" Jamie called, her voice craggy and pillow-muffled.

Tor Enberg, secluded behind his sunglasses of deep-sea green, said little as the limousine navigated the morning traffic. The band was headed to the museum for an acoustic gig to accompany the exhibit's opening. His band mates jabbered away, their necks craning to study the skyscrapers, their cameras flashing. Their rushed CD was a modest success; their US tour well attended. When they kicked into "Poor, Poor Vladimir," the others in the group danced and jumped about, but the song—and increasingly, his band mates—had begun to weigh upon Tor. Last night at the hotel bar, he'd confessed this to their manager, who surprised Tor by replying he'd been thinking the same thing and that perhaps now was the time to go solo. He was the real artist, their manager said, the songwriter. The others were simply local musicians, decent chaps for jamming and beer drinking, but here, in the heart of the music scene, their naiveté was glaring, embarrassing even. Olaf couldn't get over the wonders of room service; Christian called his girlfriend every night, whispering love-sick baby talk. Tor considered the others and understood they weren't cut out for this. He would tell them soon; they could return to the University with a modest windfall, finish their degrees and rejoin the normal lives for which they were destined. There would be hard feelings, but in the end, Tor would be doing them a favor. The limo pulled up to the museum. When the crowds on the sidewalks tried to peer into the tinted glass, Erik rolled down his window and snapped their picture. "Hello, Los Angeles!" he cried.

Connor, having survived the entrance's shouting throng, strode through the museum. His assistant handed him a phone, a studio exec pitching a role in an upcoming comic-to-movie blockbuster. The phone pressed to his ear, Connor entered the exhibit's room. Knots of officials and security studied him. He stooped to Lenin's eye level, his thighs brushing the velvet rope as the exec prattled on about the exploding Asian market. Through the coffin's glass, Connor spotted two men striding purposely toward him.

Valentin and his interpreter neared the movie star. Valentin extended his hand and, through his interpreter, introduced himself. Valentin recognized the lingering effects of alcohol and incomprehension in the other man's eyes. He shook his head. Sobriety was little more than a fashion statement in the US. Let them come to Russia and meet men who really drank. The two posed for the cameras, the star's handshake clammy and weak. Dmitri stood at the periphery, his hands clasped behind him. Valentin wondered if he'd ever seen the ghoul smile.

Tor, guided by his manager, joined the other men before the tomb. He brushed by Valentin, heartily clasped Phelps' hand, and, despite his distaste for *The Littlest Soldier*, declared himself "a big fan." Tor removed his sunglasses as the cameras flashed. His band mates lingered near the dour little man in the dark suit.

Outside, a TV crew interviewed Reverend Underwood, but his responses were drowned by his rabid mass. The plan had been for Underwood to try to gain entrance to the museum, an act of civil disobedience intended to be more symbolic than confrontational.

Underwood ducked beneath the barricade. The cameras rolled. He was scared, yes, but alive with purpose. His steady steps faltered when the barricades crashed behind him, and before he reached the curb, he was swarmed by the followers who no longer heeded his words. "Godless, worthless, and dead!" they shouted, a chant that ebbed back and forth with, "Murderer! Murderer! Murderer!" The shoving erupted when their contingent reached the museum's security detail. The Reverend beckoned for calm before a wielded sign knocked the glasses from his face.

The first dignitaries filed into the museum. Tor and his band strummed the Russian-influenced folk songs they'd been practicing. Tor studied the line making its way to the coffin, the beautiful people in this land of sun. This, he thought, was where he belonged. The paparazzi rushed the door to record the entrance of Phelps' beautiful costar from *Lenin!* Tor bungled a chord, distracted when she looked his way. He composed himself and wondered if his manager could arrange an introduction.

Connor studied her, too, amazed how quickly she could pull herself together. His manager came to his side, his phone pressed against his chest. "Your wife," he said.

His costar blew him a kiss. "I'll call her back," Connor said.

Valentin grinned as the gift shop rang up its first sale.

An alarm sounded, a cry so piercing that many ducked and covered their ears. Tor and the others stopped playing. The film crews turned their attention from Connor and Jamie's posing to the stampede that had burst through the doors. The security detail rushed forward. Reverend Underwood, half blind without his glasses, pushed to the crowd's front and placed himself between the mob and the glass coffin. He was joined by Valentin, the two men shouting in different languages: Valentin hurling guttural threats, Underwood appealing for peace.

With a hiss, one of the guards doused the front line of protestors with pepper spray. Bedlam erupted. The protestors clutched their eyes and throats, and as they staggered back, their places were taken by the rush of those behind them. Both Valentin and Underwood were pushed to the floor. The protestors swarmed the guards, and the pepper spray was now turned upon the men in uniform and anyone else who dared come close. Jamie buried her pretty face into Connor's chest. The siren died, the room now a cauldron of angry shouts. The cameramen recorded the chaos. The beautiful socialites of Los Angeles fled. Tor and his band clutched their mute instruments.

Four of the protestors, men in respectable Sunday suits and US flags pinned to their lapels, massed on one side of the coffin. With a synchronized heave of their shoulders, they rocked the pedestal. Others surrounded them, their placards swung in threatening arcs. A gash opened on Valentin's forehead, the blood running into his eye. Tor picked a woman's discarded scarf, and kneeling next to the dazed Valentin, pressed the cloth against his wound. "Stop! Stop this in the name of God!" screamed Underwood, but his voice was no match for the cries of "Murderer! Murderer!"

The glass shattered when the coffin struck the floor. A thousand jagged shards fanned over the tiles, and the sound, violent and brief, was followed by a breathy silence. The body lay in the pose of a forgotten doll, face down, one arm twisted beneath the torso, the legs crossed at the ankles. The protestors drew back, their chants abandoned. Tor helped Valentin to his feet, and they joined Connor and Reverend Underwood at the fore of the circle surrounding the body.

A small man muscled his way through the throng, barking a single Russian word as he pushed aside the protestors. Connor turned to the others. "What's he saying?"

Tor, still pressing the bloody scarf to Valentin's temple, said, "I think he's calling us animals."

Dmitri crouched beside the corpse. With great care, he turned the body over and brushed away the glass. He slid one arm beneath the neck, another under the knees. He clutched the limp form to his chest and whispered into the corpse's ear, his tears wetting the waxy skin. Dmitri lifted his head and returned every gaze aimed his way. *Animals,* he hissed in his native tongue. *Animals.*

THE PLATE SPINNER

The plate spinner stepped onto the stage. Beyond the footlight's glare, the clink of glasses. Tipsy murmurings. A woman's shrill laugh. The audience lost in a dark sea, the plate spinner alone on his island of light. He told jokes as he unlatched his trunk. The lumberjack and the milkmaid, the pool boy and the bored heiress—but his timing was off, the punch lines flat. Grumblings from the dark. The woman's laugh again, drunk and choking with stupidity. In the plate spinner's thoughts, the panic of nakedness despite his red blazer and black bowtie, the stage disorienting without his assistant. He retrieved a stack of plates and tossed the first high into the smoky air.

They'd always started with a juggling bit, the plate spinner and his assistant. His lover. Six years together, a bond deeper than the vows they'd never bothered to exchange, a marriage to the stage and the life. They'd chosen this underworld of clubs and bars and ten-dollar scams. They'd chosen the road over mortgages and backyards. They'd chosen each other. Somewhere along the line, he'd lost his grip on what held them together. This morning he woke in a dingy motel, his arms empty. A note on the dresser.

The plates flew around him. Their round faces cascaded through the light, an illusion of moon phases circling his head, their flight fueled by reflex and memory. The three-piece house band lurched into a lazy accompaniment. In the wings, the Flandreau twins adjusted each other's ostrich-plumed headdresses. They were the night's stars. Soon, they'd hoof their clumsy steps. Piece by piece, their clothes would hit the stage. Their pretty faces and young flesh would shine like jewels, the club's dim spaces rippling with longing and desire.

One of the twins tugged her spangled bikini top and adjusted her breasts. Her sequins shone, and in the breath-wide cleaving of light, the plate spinner's lover appeared. Her gaze was as it had once been, familiar, welcoming, their eyes locked as the plates flew between them. A nod, the wordless shorthand of lovers and performers, and they dared each other with the Saint Louis Loop, the dicey Hungarian Weave. Sweat glistened on their brows, their bodies united with rhythm and purpose.

A plate slid through his fingers. His lover's image dissolved, a curl of smoke consumed by the dark. The plate shattered, an odd and beautiful sacrifice at his feet. He reached out, grasping nothing, the spell broken. He covered his head as the world fell apart around him.

THE WOLF

Pines and oaks line the narrow road. Glide through the shadows like the fish you hope to catch. Little has changed in the thirty years since your first visit to the cabin. Reality measuring up to memory—it doesn't happen often. Your ten-year-old son sits beside you. Back home, he plays soccer and video games. He has a green belt in karate and edits animations on the computer. He is not excited about the trip, but he is a good sport. On the roadside, the season's first wildflowers.

Your childhood memories of the cabin: the woodpile's hairy spiders; the musty blankets you woke beneath. In the company of your father and uncles, you, too, were considered a man. You struck the blue-tip matches that ignited the barbecue. You fired a long-barreled .22 and gutted fish. At the nightly fire, you studied the whiskey glass your father held, his grip loosening the more he drank. Inevitably, he sloshed a few drops onto his lap and echoed a favorite line: "Gail will have my head!" You tossed pine cones into the flames, thrilled by the short-lived glow of burning pitch.

* * *

Another snapshot undisturbed: the lake's bait shop, its gravel lot and weather-beaten wood, its insides cramped and dim. The owner rises, a pained straightening of a body not long for this world. You wonder if he remembers you or perhaps discerns your ghost in your son's eyes. He suggests wax worms because the crappies have been biting; minnows for the walleye. As you pay, he warns of the wolf that's prowled the lakeshore this past winter.

Take the packed-dirt road to the cabin. The trees thicker here, the scent of pine. The lowest branches scrape your roof. Vegetation blurs the structure in the clearing. The grass stands shin-high. Jasmine veins the chimney. Your grandfather built this cabin. He is gone, and as of last year, so is your father. Your brother lives halfway across the country. Recently, you've been discussing selling the cabin. The decision, he says, is not his, for the cabin's maintenance would fall to you. Through the trees, the sun glimmers upon the lake.

Your son helps carry provisions inside. Open the windows and let the place breathe. Flick the main breaker. Turn the kitchen spigots until the water runs clear. Knock a hornets' nest from the porch ceiling. No one has been here in a year, maybe two. It's not hard to imagine the place melting into a tangle of saplings and vines.

Tackle box and fishing poles in tow, you head to the water. You pat your son's back, missing the boy who unthinkingly reached for your hand. The rowboat sits by the water, overturned and camouflaged by a tarp and tall grass. Pull back the tarp, exposing the turtle-like shell of ancient wood. Flipping the boat takes greater effort than you expected, and both you and your son stagger back when the field mice flee their disturbed home.

* * *

Allow your boy to settle into the stern. Your turn next, a less-than-graceful balancing act. Your son grips the boat's sides. Lock the oars into the rusted locks, and with a few strokes, reunite yourself with the physics of rowing. Another reunion waits when you clear the pines'shadows, the light of open water, its sheen and rhythm. How could you have forgotten something so beautiful? Your son faces you as the shoreline fades behind him.

Row to the shady cove your father loved. Buttonballs from the sycamores bob around you. Your son's hand trails through the water, boomerang ripples in his wake. Help your boy bait his hook, and the memory of your father's hands comes to you. The excitement of your boy's first strike justifies the day's headaches. With a hoist of the bent rod, he deposits the walleye in the hull. The fish flips, its mouth puckering, a slow drowning in the spring air. For the next three hours, you cast and reel. Release the small ones, cupping them in the water until they swim off, their fins tickling your palms.

Return to the bait shop for charcoal. The evening air turns crisp. You hadn't notice the owner's holstered pistol before. He says if you brought a dog to keep him inside tonight. The wolf killed two dogs last month. "Do you have yourself a gun?" he asks.

Four fish hang from your stringer. Stifling your squeamishness, you cut the fish from jaw to tail and remove the internal organs. Your son offers to gut the last walleye. The knife trembles in his grip, but you swallow back the advice you want to offer. As the fish fry over open flames, you toss the guts into the trees. The charcoal glows under the darkening sky.

* * *

Wipe dust from the checkerboard, buttons and shell casings taking the place of the missing pieces. Try your son's hand-held computer game, but your skills are no match for his. Lie in the cot beside your son and discuss your plans for tomorrow. The sun's warmth lingers on your face, your shoulders sore from rowing. You remind him he can talk to you about anything, anytime; he says he knows. He falls asleep, and before you leave, you steal a stroke of his cheek.

The bourbon waits in the top kitchen cabinet. Pour a few fingers in a glass. The liquid warms your throat. You're not much of a drinker, but tonight you feel an allegiance to roles both abandoned and inherited. From the distance comes the wolf's baleful cry, and only now do you think of the fish guts you tossed in the woods. Go to the window, but the glass holds little more than your faint reflection.

Colder now. Lay an extra blanket over your sleeping boy and wrap another around your shoulders. The wolf howls again, closer this time. Sit in your father's chair, glass in hand, and consider the empty room.

THE HUNTER

B eneath the covers, the boy held a flashlight to his hand. The bones of his fingers a leafless tree, his flesh sunset red. He turned the flashlight to the book by his side. *Gray's Anatomy*, a volume rescued from the library's annual sale. *Withdrawn* stamped on its title page. The boy flipped past images of skulls and spinal columns before stopping at a picture of a hand. In the drawing, the skin had been removed, revealing a textured landscape of muscles and tendons. The boy opened his drawing pad and began to sketch.

In the woods, he shot groundhogs and rabbits and squirrels. He used his father's .22. His father had drowned last spring. When the boy held the rifle's sights on a living creature, his breath stilled and his heartbeat swimming in his ears, his father seemed close. The boy had grown into a patient hunter, and he believed his father would have been proud.

On a frigid January morning, the boy killed a hare, a clean shot through the head. The echo lingered amid the bare branches, and the boy's boots crunched over the brush. Time was of the essence. He rolled the hare onto its back and used his mother's five-inch hatpins to anchor the paws to the earth. His knife's honed blade hissed as it cut from crotch to jaw. The dusting of snow beneath the hare turned red. He made two more cuts, groin to hip, jaw to shoulder, and then peeled back the fur. Steam rose from the carcass, and the boy leaned close, knowing this mist was like no other. He took the sketchpad from his backpack. His pencil scratched the paper, his pace quickening as the steam faded.

THE NEST

The girl sat by her bedroom window. Morning light sifted through the sycamore. The goldfinch hopped along a limb and chattered its nervous song. The girl whistled back. For the past two weeks, the goldfinch had been weaving its nest in the azalea bush beneath the girl's window. The bird scurried back and forth, acrobatic flashes of yellow and black, grasses and twigs snared in its stubby beak. The girl checked the nest's progress every day. What had begun as a straggly mass was now a tightly woven bowl tucked deep beneath the azalea's fading blooms.

The goldfinch abandoned its song. The bird cocked its head, a rare moment of pause, then took to the air. Before the girl could stand, the tremors hit. The trophies and pictures atop her dresser jiggled. A pencil rolled across her desk. The girl closed her eyes. The upheaval resonated in her bones, her hands locked upon the chair's sides. Ten seconds, then stillness. The girl breathed again. The goldfinch returned to its song.

The girl stepped into the narrow upstairs hallway. She was eleven, old enough to look after herself on a Saturday morning. She no longer cried when the Earth shook. The hinges of her parents' bedroom door sighed. Her mother, still wearing last night's dress, lay sprawled across the bed. The shoes the girl had slipped off sat neatly on the floor. The girl stepped forward, her body stirring the haze of cigarettes and whiskey. She held a hand above her mother's mouth. Her breath's moist current curled against the girl's palm.

Downstairs, the girl fixed herself toast. Wisps of sawdust littered the linoleum by the backdoor. Her father had been by last night to put in new locks. The girl had sat with him, handing him the tools he asked for. The locks were heavy, thick deadbolts, the girl's reflection warped in the polished brass. There had been a man on the moon. There had been murder in the canyon. There had been murder in the city, a house little different than hers. Fear on the gritty breeze. Her father had installed the locks but didn't stay the night. An argument before he left, exchanges that shook the walls, their venom and vanities chasing the girl from the room. The Earth split beneath her feet. Her head white with static. A panic in her chest, a drowning miles from the ocean.

A sleepover last week. A flashlight game, voices in the dark. Her girlfriend whispering in her ear: "They cut the baby out of her. Alive."

The girl placed her dish in the sink and went outside. The sun low. Chill in the shadows. The goldfinch's serenade. The girl shielded her eyes and whistled back. The bird masked by the sycamore's leaves. Above, a blue sky, another beautiful day.

She went to the azalea bush. The dew cooled her bare feet. She nudged aside the branches. In the nest, three small eggs, oblong and pale and faintly speckled. The girl had been wondering when or if. The goldfinch cried. The girl pulled back, leaves rustling, when she noticed the other egg.

She froze. The egg lay perched upon a nexus of leafless shoots. Perhaps the tremor had shaken it loose. Perhaps the goldfinch, sensing rot or death, had nudged it from the nest. The girl reached into the bush. Dying blooms drifted to the ground. She knew once she touched the egg, she couldn't return it, her human scent a stain that wouldn't fade. The egg shifted, a hiccupping tumble between the shoots. The girl lurched forward, the branches scratching her hand, and snared the egg.

She pulled the egg from the bush. The shell lay cool and smooth against her skin. A cut on the back of her hand, a trickle of blood. She thought of the life that waited beneath the shell. She lifted her gaze to the sycamore. The goldfinch twittered. The girl's mother appeared in the bedroom window. The sun's glare a cool fire in the glass, her mother a bloodless mirage, a ghost eclipsed by a lowered shade.

The girl considered the egg. She thought of the pictures sent from space, the Earth a swirl of pale clouds. There had been a time she'd cried when the ground shook, but she was older than that now. She cupped the egg, a slow ratcheting of pressure. A soft crack, then a spider web of thin fissures. The goldfinch circled above, wings flapping.

The Couple and Their Secrets

He'd killed a man, a friend who'd betrayed him. The body weighed with chains and cinder blocks. The moon's reflection cupped in dark water. An oar's slap, muddy crust on his boots, a tarp unfurled. Thirty years had passed, and what pained him most were these details, each a seed, each a poison flower.

She'd had a lover in college, a boy she barely recognized in the light of day. An abortion at twenty. With her husband, she had a daughter, and swimming in her girl's eyes, a ghost child unborn.

On their property, a hundred-year oak. In the tree's sundown shadows, they discovered comfort they would never confess, their sins dwarfed by this witness destined to outlive them both.

When would peace find them? If they only knew the secret they shared—that each pictured their last breath beneath a cold November moon, a cloud here, then not.

THE TWINS

At birth, the boy's umbilical cord lassoed his sister's neck. The girl was born blue and cold. By the age of ten, she'd been asked to leave school. In the classroom, she ate crayons and whooped during morning prayers. On the playground, she pulled up her dress. The principal called her a simpleton. He didn't mean to be cruel. Things were different then. The twins' mother cried. The girl's fingers twitched like frightened birds.

If anyone teased the girl, her brother punched them in the mouth without a word of warning. He even fought the older boys who smoked stolen cigarettes behind the schoolyard fence. Black eyes and bloody noses only fueled the boy's rage. In time, the other children fell silent when the boy and his babbling sister passed.

The twins lived on a farm outside town. There was always work to do. The boy often tied one end of a rope around his sister's waist and the other around his. She had a tendency to wander—into the fields, down to the creek—called by voices her brother would never hear. The boy and his family would waste the rest of the day calling her name and stumbling through thistles or muddy fields or August's killing heat. When they found her, she'd study them with the eyes of a woken dreamer.

The boy was angry when he learned he couldn't go to school the day before Christmas break. Their mother had to tend to a sick relative in town. The boy would stay home and mind his sister. The boy would miss his teacher's pecan cookies. He wouldn't get to unwrap the dime-store whistles and tin cars she bought for her students. When their mother left, the boy cursed his sister. His sister made gurgling noises and stuck her fingers in her mouth. The boy called her the names that would have started a fight had anyone else said them. His sister stared. The boy cursed her a final time and crumbled into tears. His sister hugged him with spit-wet hands and cooed her nonsense into his ear.

The boy had been told to clean the loft. His sister followed him outside, but it was her brother who fetched and zipped her coat. She picked up the rope and handed it to him. He said no. She handed it to him again and smiled her lopsided smile. The boy sighed and knotted the rope around their waists.

The boy climbed the loft's ladder first. His sister followed. The dust lay thick on the floor's knotted planks. Spider webs clung to the rafters. Wind whistled between the laths. The boy's sister had climbed the ladder hundreds of times, but this morning, just as her face crested the loft's edge, she slipped. The tug slammed the boy to the floor. He skidded on his backside, the friction burning his skin. The beam that saved him from falling knocked the wind from his gut. He gazed over the edge. Suspended halfway between the loft and the floor, his sister twisted at the rope's end. She looked up, perplexed at first, then waved.

The boy struggled to prop his feet against the beam. Hand over hand, he pulled her up. For every tug, the rope slipped a bit. His fingers blistered. His shoulders burned. Finally, her hands grasped the loft's floor. He reached out to her. This, he figured, was how it would always be between them.

THE TRAIN

Study the night sky. Let your focus wander. Let the stars come to you. Close your eyes, and entertain the afterimages. A thousand suns shine for you alone.

You lie half naked and sweating on the wooden dock. Moonless, the pond as black as the sky. Pitiless August. Crickets, cicadas, bullfrogs—the night throbs with their songs. Hands clasped across your chest, you hold a smoldering punk. The tip glows. Smoke curls toward the stars. An ashy column tumbles onto your skin.

You are the youngest of four. One brother carries a machine gun through a country of heat and dust. Your sister left college with a teaching degree and a mountain of debt. Another brother languishes in jail, a victim of bad temper and worse luck. Sit up. In the distance, your house, the lights fragmented by the willows. Soon you, too, must leave.

No breeze cools you; the water slimy with algae. In the distance, a train whistle. Two hundred yards from where you sit, the tracks run along your property. Tremors in the dock's crooked planks.

Run barefoot through the sea of wildflowers and knee-high grass. Crickets fan out, husky pecks against your legs. The heat a wet veil you can't break. The train louder now, the Doppler rush of compressed waves, a warping of the physical world, a compression echoed in your gut. Faster now, you and the train, the headlamp slicing into the night. The engine's call drowns the bugs, the frogs, your racing heart. Scramble up the stony rail bed as the train nears.

The lamp's shine blinds you, then darkness again. Spread your arms. Savor the sooty gale. Deafening, the roar, the clatter of steel wheels, an earthly thunder that shakes every part of you. The cars rush past, their sides colored with graffiti from distant cities. Lose yourself in the violence of a world in motion.

Just as quickly, the train is gone. In its place, silence. The heat. The darkness. The open view of the fields you've known all your life.

THE DOGS, THE DOGS

Susan loved Eric because he was damaged like her. He'd grown up uncertain and wild, the way motherless boys often do. Cancer had taken Susan's father the winter before, and with his passing, Susan joined the demographic of the left behind, a tribe who understood absence was more than an empty chair at the kitchen table. Susan struggled to accept her burden with a believer's mute strength, but on their first date, Eric toed the quarry's sheer ridge and cursed the God Susan so feared. Her heart, having been bluffed by a lifetime of sermons, finally recognized itself in that pit of echoes and stones.

A hot summer, cicadas first, then the crickets, the darkness throbbing as Eric and Susan lay naked beneath the hundred-year-old oak that grew at the edge of her farmhouse lot. The breeze from the alfalfa blew moist and thick. Moonshine on the oak's shimmying leaves. Susan always took a moment to kiss the pink scar on Eric's shoulder, the reminder of a knife fight his first week in juvenile hall. This was how they loved, their gentlest selves offered to the other's imperfections, their healing wishes heaped upon each other's scars. Some nights, they'd return to the quarry, her voice joining his, a sound too full of life and hurt to be held by this earth. A cry rising to the stars.

They were once connected, Susan and her mother, linked by blood and tissue in a force truer than any New Testament miracle. Her arms were Susan's refuge from nightmares and thunderstorms, but after her husband died, Susan's mother surrendered to a selective blindness, one in which Susan's well-being meant less than it once did. Widowed, living in a country house that had been in her husband's family for generations, her mother crumbled. Predicted blizzards cast her into a tizzy. She couldn't sleep when the squirrels chased each other in the attic. She cried when the toilet overflowed. She retreated into a haze of prayer, her faith insulating her like a drug.

Paul Hughes sang alongside her in the church choir. He was also the county sheriff, his cruiser always parked in the fire lane just outside the vestibule doors. On a firefly-sparkling night, he visited after practice. He sipped from the iced tea glass Susan's mother never let run dry, and the two of them bonded over favorite hymns and the decline of American morals. Susan's mother couldn't replace a fuse, but she knew how to wait on a man. Summer faded into autumn, and as Paul made trips to sample fresh blueberry cobbler or fix the trash disposal, Susan discovered herself growing invisible in her mother's eyes, the flesh-and-blood her eclipsed by the mirror reflection her mother ran to check each time Paul's cruiser trundled down their lane. "Paul says you should stay away from that boy," Susan's mother warned. They had a history, Paul and Eric, Paul the arresting officer after Eric torched the car of the man who'd given his sister a black eye. "He says Eric and his family are trouble." Susan didn't answer, convinced all her mother knew about love could be pissed into a thimble.

* * *

They married beneath the hundred-year oak. A cold snap had dashed Susan's mother's spring-wedding dreams, and Susan shivered in the bridesmaid dress she'd sewn, her bouquet's petals and the preacher's words carried off on a numbing wind. After returning from their Aruba honeymoon to find a pair of boxers beneath Susan's bed, Paul banned Eric from visiting. "I can't tell you who to date," he said, "but I can tell you who can and can't enter my house."

"Your house?" Susan asked.

Susan readied herself for work. Deep July. Dust in the fields, the roadside macadam gummy. Not a breeze all day. Susan checked herself in the mirror. Ahead waited a ten-hour shift, her fifth this week. She had her regular hours, then the others she took for coworkers vacationing or tending to children. Her paychecks went to insurance and gas, the old compact car that was once her father's now hers. Outside, the baying of Paul's hunting hound, the beast driven mad by the groundhogs that prowled the field's edges. The dog rushed toward a rustling in the weeds. Its chain snapped, its bark snuffed into a pained yelp.

Downstairs, Susan slipped into her supermarket apron. She ate a bowl of cereal as she stood over the kitchen sink. Her mother knelt amid the garden's leafed rows, zucchini and squash, the watermelons growing fat. Her mother had landed safely in life's next act, a housewife content in her garden. Susan tried to be happy for her, but she couldn't. It all stank of betrayal. Not to Susan—she wasn't a child any longer—but to what had been. To the life they'd made in this house.

A rifle's crack, a shock of blue-sky thunder. The bowl slipped from Susan's hand. Milk and cereal splashed in the sink. Susan grabbed her wallet, her passing reflection captured in the gun cabinet's glass. Her flat-soled shoes hurried across the lawn's dandelions. The keys dangled from the ignition. The compact's shocks weren't what they should be, and the car bucked up the rutted drive. Paul stood erect on his makeshift range, bare-chested, his gut straining over his belt, tinted glasses and plugs in his ears. He worked the bolt and raised his beloved Mauser. Another trigger squeeze, and a bottle shattered twenty yards downrange. Susan's car fishtailed onto the road, tires squealing on the macadam, her foot heavy on the gas, her gaze on the rearview until the farmhouse disappeared.

A busy Saturday at the grocery checkout. Susan's conveyor belt in constant motion, a parade of cereals and meats and fruits, magazines and candy and pet food. A hundred customers passed before her first break, faces flushed with sun, children in squeaking flip-flops. Susan chatted with old teachers; with church members who asked after her mother and Paul. Then the nameless others—women pregnant and not, the herders of rowdy broods. The meticulous coupon-clippers. The frazzled. The rude. The kind. The flirting boys and creepy men.

Money came and went, a brushing of fingers, Susan an exile behind the glaze of good manners. *Yes, sir. No, ma'am. Have a nice weekend.* On days like this, she felt the way she did when she stood riverside, a sensation of stillness as so much flowed past. She considered the faces, each a reflection of what might be. Pregnant, yes, children. Old, her wrinkled fingers fishing through her change purse. She could not make up her mind whether this was beautiful or sad.

The sun had set by the time her shift ended. Heat radiated from the macadam. The parking lot's dark fringe, the wink of headlights from Eric's van, a welcome as Susan shrugged off her apron. She climbed inside. His kiss tasted of sun and soap, his face warm from his day's work, the landscaping gig that kept him hustling from morning to sundown. On his fingers, the stubborn grease from his tinkering, the van's engine temperamental and in continual need of fixing. Baron, the terrier mutt Eric had rescued, clambered onto Susan's lap. Its sandpaper tongue wet her chin.

They drove out of town. The river road empty. Stifling in the van, the heat pumping to save the engine from overheating. They passed a gas station, a speck of light, a momentary shimmering across their sweat-gleaming faces. Through the trees, glimpses of the river.

Eric pulled onto a dirt spur, a leafy aperture Susan would have been pressed to find in broad daylight. Ten yards in, he stopped the van. Swatting back the bugs that crowded the headlights' shine, he wrestled aside a rusty chain. This riverside plot was his grandfather's, a man whose senility had left him childlike, the property left to be claimed by brambles and vines. Eric climbed back in. The dash's lights shone orange in his eyes. The brush grew thicker, the road a pair of parallel tracks through the ferns and mayapples. Tall trees blotted out the stars, and beneath, a tangle of sun-starved saplings.

They stopped in a small clearing. The river opened before them, a half-mile swath of moonlit ripples. Susan listened to the voluminous push as certain as the blood in her veins. A stone put-in area sloped to the water's edge. A weathered cabin, its roof speckled with leaves and moss, anchored the clearing's far end. Baron leapt from Susan's opened door, a scramble across the clearing, his stubby tail wagging as he nipped at the fireflies. Eric led Susan to the van's rear. Kneeling, they undressed each other. Susan blind, her world defined by touch alone until her eyes adjusted enough to discern the bands of white skin they shared with no one else.

Afterward, they did not speak, both of them dizzy with uncirculated air and content to savor the bliss they'd claimed from the night. Through the roof's cracked vent came the hint of honeysuckle and an owl's hoot and the river's unyielding rumble. Susan rested her hand on Eric's damp chest. In her fingers, the beat of his heart, the rise of his lungs, their currents in harmony with the rhythms all around them. Eric tickled her nose with Baron's chew-toy, a length of thick, knotted rope. Susan asked him to trace the rope's frayed end over her body. Her skin tightened beneath the touch.

The van's opened vent yawned toward the unbothered stars. The plastic cupped the moonlight, a milky halo over their heads. Susan raised her hand. The faintest breeze touched her skin. They began to speak, a revisiting of their budding plans to leave all this behind and start anew in the Florida town where Eric had spent the happiest years of his nomadic childhood. He talked of palm trees and warm sand and the taste of the fish he and his uncle had grilled over an open fire. He made it sound like paradise. *Yes, yes*, Susan said, *let's go.*

Summer's final week, Susan's senior year about to begin. Steam rose from the cup she carried to Paul. Her mother, who'd brewed the coffee and insisted Susan deliver the cup, watched from the kitchen window. The drive's gravel scraped beneath Susan's sneakers. In the open space behind the barn where her father had grazed his goats, Paul had erected a large pen. The breeze shifted, and on it, the stink of wet fur. In the past few months, Paul had bought six more hounds. They were dull creatures, their reasoning shackled to instinct, master, and chase. Their glistening snouts poked between the wire.

Paul set down the fence roll he was stringing to the posts of a smaller pen. He took the coffee. The shadow of his baseball cap masked his eyes. Susan glanced over his shoulder, remembering how her father's goats had shambled though the clover and the lazy ring of the bell strung around their buck's neck.

"Could use a little help," he said

He slurped and handed Susan the cup. The gurgle of liquid in his mouth, his mustache's damp tips—these were the latest suffocating notes the hymn-singer had brought into her life. Her father had been buried once, and now Paul was burying him again, with his interloper's thudding footfalls and post-dinner belches. With the oily scent of the guns he cleaned at the kitchen table and the whiskers he left in the sink. With the stifled grunts he wheezed from behind her mother's bedroom door.

The dogs wedged between each other, a shifting, snapping mass. One knocked over a feeding dish. The others answered with frenzied barks.

"Quiet!" Paul snapped. The dogs shrank back from the fence.

The fencing stood five feet high, a grid of plastic-coated wire. Susan set down the cup and pulled the heavy roll tight while Paul secured metal ties to the post. He huffed with each twist of his pliers.

"You getting more dogs?" she asked.

"One more. This will be a breeding pen." He yanked the roll past the next post. His coffee-flavored breath broke over Susan's face. "I've got a connection in Kentucky. I'm buying a bitch with all the right papers." He grinned as he handed her the roll. She could tell he got a thrill from saying *connection* and *bitch*. "I'm going to raise the finest hounds from here to the state line."

Susan considered the patch of dirt and grass behind the wire. "So that's all she'll do? Have pups her whole life in this pen?"

"There's worse ways for a dog to live."

"I guess."

He grunted as he attached another tie. "That's life, honey."

Susan looked away from the pale crescent that peeked above his sagging belt. "Don't call me honey, Paul."

The congregation sat. The hard-backed pew forced Susan's spine to attention. With pinching fingers, she harvested black and brown hairs from her lap and cursed

Paul's hounds again. In the pew in front of her, a baby cried. His mother held him, his face above her shoulder, his expression contorted with a pain no embrace could soothe. "Hush," his mother whispered.

Paul strode to the altar's center, the spot once occupied by Susan's father's coffin. The organist played the first, strident notes of "The Blood-Washed Pilgrim," a tune Paul and her mother had been humming all week. The sun broke. Colored shafts slanted into the gray space, the stained-glass banishment of Adam and Eve suddenly alive. A sluggish yellow jacket tapped the glass then fell to the window ledge. Paul sang of blood and the lamb, of believers who faced the pit and the fire. What he lacked in range, he atoned for in volume, the refrains booming, his voice battling the child's uncomforted wailings. Paul held his hymnal in one hand, his other rising to the heavens. The shifting contours of his golden robe betrayed the pistol strapped around his waist.

October, the hills at their most colorful. The hounds swarmed when Susan ducked into the pen. They were thirsty, and being dogs, all they understood was the moment's thirst may as well have been forever's. Susan stooped, the pen too small for her to stand. The buckets' weight tugged her from side to side. The nearest dogs plunged their snouts into the water. The others howled and nipped, and before Susan could rest the buckets, her jeans had become soaked. She stepped back, and the hounds rushed forward, a jostling kaleidoscope of stupidity and need.

One of the beasts lifted his head, his snout dripping, a pose swiftly mimicked by the others. Paul's truck appeared at the end of the lane. The pen erupted in howls. The finches pecking at the lane's shallow puddles took to the sky. Paul had been gone two days, a trip to retrieve the breeder he believed would make him rich. Susan's mother exited the kitchen, her hands smoothing her apron. Paul cut the engine and climbed from the cab. Bedlam seized the cage, and Paul, after hugging Susan's mother, extended a hand through the pen's wire. The dogs battled to lap his fingers.

"Well," Susan's mother said, "let's see her."

Reaching into the bed, Paul loosened the straps and slid the carrier onto the opened gate.

The dogs whimpered. Paul unlatched the cage. "Come on, girl." He snapped his fingers. "Don't be scared now."

He groped into the carrier, but then cursed and yanked back his arm. The bite, tiny as it was, drew blood, a thin stream along his pinkie. He reached back into the cage and, grabbing the bunched fur behind her neck, pulled the dog onto the gate. The dog trembled, her tail tucked between her legs, her head bowed and her long ears masking her face. A stream of piss trickled onto the gate's vinyl lining.

Paul set her on the ground. In the pen, two dogs turned on each other. Paul shouted, but the dogs refused to heed. He snatched the hose Susan had used to fill the buckets and sprayed until the fighters beat a whimpering retreat.

"It's her scent." Paul turned the stream onto his bit hand and washed off the blood. "They'll be used to her in no time."

Susan's mother knelt and stroked the dog's head. "She's a beauty."

"That she is." Paul wiped his hands against his jeans. "And she's ready to breed."

Susan's mother lifted the dog's chin. "What're you going to call her?"

Paul turned to Susan. "Thought you'd like to name her."

Susan studied the dog. "I don't know."

Paul smiled. "It will come to you."

Susan stepped onto the back porch. The blizzard had been raging since morning, a sea of white, her car buried beneath a rounded heap. She pulled up her jacket's hood. The light was fading, the snow predicted to keep up until midnight. Then more wind, the temperatures plummeting. The interstate shut down. Livestock warnings on the radio.

She made her way toward the barn. Not a trace remained of the path she and Paul had shoveled after lunch. Knee-high drifts, snow in her boots. The sagging wires that connected house to barn swayed. The cold raked her skin, her gaze down, her path veering. She kicked back the drift that had climbed up the barn door. Her feet planted wide, she tugged the rusted latch. The entry just wide enough to slip inside.

The barn's foundation dated back to the late 1800's, and the dogs' barks echoed off the thick veins of mortar, the stones of gray and brown. Naked bulbs hung from the rafters, and the watery shine shuddered with each gust. Paul had herded the dogs into the straw-lined pen where her father had once cared for his sick goats. Outside the pen, a kerosene heater burned, an oily stink that mingled with the scent of shit and piss, the heater's current not enough to keep the dogs' water bowls from icing. The dogs slobbered and bayed. The steam of their breath a haze above the pen. Susan broke the bowls' ice and filled the food dishes.

She stepped back out. Darker now. A blue tint over the snowy fields. Tears in her eyes, the wind stealing her breath. Deep drifts in their lane. Come tomorrow, the sheriff's office would send a detail for Paul, a snowmobile perhaps, the spectacle fueling Paul's self-importance. Susan and her mother stranded until one of Susan's uncles plowed their lane.

Inside the kitchen, Susan set her boots next to Paul's. The feeling returned to her face and hands. Her mother at the stove, steam from a boiling pot, a roast in the oven. Good smells overwhelmed by the stink of gun oil. Towels on the kitchen table, the gun cabinet doors swung open.

Paul's oiled rag glided along a blue-steel barrel. He hummed, and Susan's mother joined in, the two of them soon singing: "What a friend we have in Jesus . . ."

Susan put on a kettle on the stove's only unclaimed burner. Paul's breeding bitch stirred from its blanketed nest by the coal stove. He'd named the dog Lucky. Susan crouched by Lucky's side and stroked her short-haired coat. She'd had her first litter, six black and tan pups, the last one sold just before the snows hit, Susan surprised by how swiftly they were claimed and by the money that had changed hands. She rested her palm on the dog's belly. Come spring, Paul would breed her again.

Paul raised the assembled rifle and gazed down the sites. "Any idea how much this is worth?"

Susan kept her back to him. "No."

"There's market value, then there's history. World War One. Lord knows what it's seen."

Paul returned the rifle to the gun cabinet and shut the door. Her mother set the table, still singing: "Everything to God in prayer." Steam plumed from the kettle. Susan let the whistle cry through the next verse before pouring her tea. At the table, Paul held her mother's hand then reached for Susan's. Her fingers disappeared in the fleshy grip, his touch delivering a chill that cut deeper than any blizzard wind.

They filled their plates. Paul dominated the conversation, digressions on liberalism and morality. Susan's mother nodded, a submissive, adoring refrain. Food clung to Paul's bushy mustache, the hairy tips dampened as he slurped his coffee. Susan kept her gaze upon her plate. She ate quickly, each bite sullied by the lingering stink of oil, her only desire to retreat to her room. She sank beneath her skin, an imperfect hush, Paul's words ignored but his gnashing teeth and damp swirl of his tongue impossible to escape.

Susan pulled her vibrating phone from her pocket and cradled it in her lap. The screen glowed in the shadows, a text from Eric: *wish i was hlding u now.* Susan's fingers tapped: *u hav no idea.*

"Put the phone away, Susan." Paul shoved a forkful of roast into his already full mouth. "There's none of that at the dinner table."

Susan slid the phone back into her pocket. Lucky trotted to her and placed her muzzle on Susan's lap. She stroked its head, its short hair bristling. Susan turned to her mother. "May I be excused?"

"You've barely touch—"

Paul interrupted: "Kids. Even the ones in youth group. Always on their phones." He wiped his mouth, another stain for his napkin. "This need for constant connection. I don't get it. We weren't like that, were we, honey?"

Susan's mother demure, a faint smile. "No."

Susan stroked the dog's shoulder. "May I please be excused?"

Lucky rested a paw on Susan's thigh. A begging whimper.

"Down, girl," Paul said.

Lucky kept her watery eyes upon Susan. She lifted another paw onto Susan's thigh and licked her cheek.

"Damn it." Paul stood. His napkin dropped to the floor. He latched onto the dog's collar, a choking tug. Lucky whimpered, front paws flailing, nails scratching the hardwood as Paul roughhoused her into her bed.

"Stay!" he bellowed. The dog set a foot onto the floor. Paul delivered a sharp blow to her snout. "Stay!"

The dog lay down. The back door slammed before Paul could reclaim his seat. Susan zippered her coat, but her boots remained unbuckled. The wind shrieked beneath the eaves. The oak's bare branches swayed. Susan stumbled through the drifts. The dogs' muffled barks carried from behind the barn doors. She staggered up the lane, the snow swelling over her thighs. A fire in her lungs. A cold sting on her face. She turned and caught her breath. Lights in the distant windows, the details blurred by the snowy gusts. Susan screamed, a rage culled from deep in her gut. Her voice tattered and kidnapped by the gale.

Susan and Eric at the riverside clearing, a pair of beach chairs pulled to the water's edge. Hats and heavy jackets, the last of the snow stubborn on roadsides and fields. A musty blanket around them. The month before, a fire at the supermarket, her paychecks gone. Paul had promised to pick up her car's insurance and pay for new shocks, but from now on, she would have to ask him for the keys. Baron on her lap. Stars. The music of water, the breeze light but icy. They each wore a glove, and Eric passed a joint from his bare hand to hers. He talked of Florida. A packed bag, a tank of gas, and they would erase all this. She lifted her chin, a lungful of smoke released to the sky. A new state. A new type of sunshine. A warmth that would never fade.

An early April Sunday. Daffodils in the garden, crocuses. The river high with snowmelt. Susan in the pews; her mother and Paul side by side in the choir. Later, an afternoon of chores, the first bees. The birds in the oak silent after each of Paul's gunshots. Susan tended to the dogs. Lucky showing the first bulge of her new litter. Paul with his Jesus-this and Jesus-that—all the while, the hungry swell in his eyes. Every Sunday the same routine, her mother and Paul retreating to the bedroom after dark. A hush, then the rhythm of bedsprings, Paul's beefy moans.

Susan on the porch, Lucky by her side. She ran a hand over Lucky's belly. The dogs in the pen howled.

Graduation night, pictures snapped, the afterimages swimming in Susan's eyes. Susan in her Sunday dress. Stiff poses, Paul fumbling with the timer. Cousins and uncles, covered dishes on the picnic table. Eric uninvited,

Susan's father barely mentioned. Lucky watching from the porch, the dog's movements stiff after miscarrying her litter, five stillborn pups buried at the alfalfa's edge.

A ceremony in the school gym, speeches Susan barely heard. The alma mater sung by the choir. A walk across the stage, a sweaty handshake from her principal and a diploma. Caps thrown into the air, a storm of blue and gold. After, Paul and her mother waiting in the parking lot, Susan sneaking off in Eric's van. Her phone to her ear, a story about going out with her girlfriends. She'd grown adept at lying. Baron on her lap, Susan trying to stifle her laugh as the dog licked her face. The light sketchy gray by the time they reached the riverside clearing.

Susan threw her suitcase onto the bed and sprung the latches. A rain-scented breeze, the window curtains' dance. The dogs howled, their master beeping in return, Paul and Susan's mother on their way to choir practice. An argument earlier at dinner, Paul dictating how the money her father had sweated for would be spent. "College only," Paul had said, a supposed echoing of her father's wishes.

Quiet in Susan's voice, a steely hiss: "Don't you dare say his name."

A flash in Paul's eyes. A reflection of the fiery pit he believed awaited her kind. Calmer heads before they left, Paul saying they'd brew a kettle and talk after tonight's practice. A silent goodbye kiss from her mother.

Susan filled the suitcase. Clothes. Toiletries. A framed picture of her father with his goats. With each packed handful, the place eased its claim, a subtracting of what was and an increase of what would be. Left behind: her soccer trophies and church clothes. Her science fair ribbons. The teddy bear she once couldn't sleep without. Dust on the cigar box atop the bookshelf. Inside, cicada shells and snake skins, wonders she'd collected alongside her father. She picked up a cicada. The honey shell crumbled. Susan made a nest amid her packed clothes for the box and framed photo.

Eric's van eased down the lane. The dogs in a frenzy. A soft click of latches, another goodbye. The suitcase's hard corners banged the stairwell's plaster. Elation in her heart, but also the heaviness of knowing today would mark another irretrievable distance. Eric beeped, Baron's high-pitched bark. Susan paused before the gun case, her reflection in the glass.

She ran across the lawn. The Mauser's strap weighed upon her shoulder. A nickel-plated Colt tucked under her arm. Eric's hand reached for the suitcase but his eyes never left the rifle. "Don't worry," Susan said. "Everything's going to be OK."

A final look as Eric closed the van door. The house that was no longer home. The oak's wet leaves shivered in the breeze. The dogs threw themselves at their cage. In the other pen, Lucky silent and watchful. They hit the road. Humid air rushed through the opened windows. Susan held the Colt in her hands. Her eyes stared back from the barrel's chrome.

Towering oaks surrounded the riverside clearing. A week, maybe ten days—that was how long Eric figured he'd need to fix the van, the parts bought after they'd sold Paul's guns. Heat blistered the valley. Mist on the morning water. Days passed, but in their shaded clearing, time belonged not to the calendar but to the river, the sun and stars. Fifty yards of forest and brush separated them from the river road, and if it weren't for the freight line that shadowed the far bank, Susan could have fooled herself into thinking she'd been cut loose from all she'd ever known.

The cabin had been claimed by mice and snakes and swifts. They slept in Eric's tent or, when the thunderstorms hit, the van. Susan gathered river stones and built a fire pit. Their drying clothes haunted the oaks' low limbs. Some mornings they woke to a bloodied mouse outside their tent flap, a tribute from Baron to his masters.

Susan, dressed in panties and one of Eric's shirts, waded into the river. Sunlight on the water, an expanse of blinding pinpoints. Parcels of mist lingered beneath the overhanging trees. Steam from the ring of stones, the embers of their morning fire. The riverbank's grasses rippled with camouflaged scurryings. Susan cast her line, a flick of the wrist, just the way her father had taught her. The current pushed against her calves. Baron splashed out, snagged a floating stick twice his size, and wrestled it back to shore. In the clearing, Eric ducked beneath the van's yawning hood, the grass around him littered with parts.

Florida, he said. The fruit on the trees just waiting to be picked. The lizards as common and benign as the north's chipmunks.

Susan's line snapped taut. The spool hissed. The rod bent, her catch ornery and full of fight. Baron abandoned his stick and stood, ear perked. Eric pulled his head from beneath the hood.

"Get him, babe!" he shouted.

Susan stepped from the tent. The morning shadows stretched over the clearing, a darkness pinholed by sunlit shafts busy with pollen and insect dances. Eric already at work, final adjustments, a few turns of the wrench and they'd be on their way. Baron bounded alongside Susan as she broke down their tent and loaded their gear into the van.

A bath before their journey. Sparrows twittered in the trees. Eric and Susan waded naked into the river. A freight train rattled along the far shore. Susan waved, hoping there was someone on board to see them, a linking to this place. Early, but already thick, the sun blazing upon the river. Silt and smooth stones beneath their feet, the water up to their bellies. The contrast between the morning's warmth and the water's cool flow made Susan feel as if she'd balanced all of nature over her body. On shore, Baron flushed a pheasant from the brush. The bird's great wings flapped, a rising into the blue, the dog barking and leaping below. Susan and Eric ventured further, taking turns to wash each others' back and hair.

Deeper still, and with the weight taken from her body, Susan embraced Eric. She wrapped her legs around his waist, an anchor against the current. Florida, yes. Soon they'd be on their way, but if it were up to Susan, she'd be just as happy if they erected a dome over this wooded clearing, a country of two where they'd be free to fish and fuck and play with their dog until they died, gray-haired and smiling.

She pushed Eric's wet bangs from his face. "Will we ever come back?"

"Only if you want."

The riverbank sparrows lit from the oaks. The sheriff's cruiser pulled into the clearing. Baron yapped and scrambled toward the car. Susan and Eric sank back, crouching until their eyes peered hippo-like above the glinting surface. Paul stepped from the cruiser, Baron's protests silenced with a swift kick. Eric clamped a hand over Susan's mouth and sidestepped them toward a crop of boulders. They hung on, peeking from behind the smooth rock. The current flowed swift around the stones, gurgles and swirling eddies.

Paul shouted toward the woods: "I know you're here! And you know I'll be back!" He ducked into the van. His arms laden with their camping gear, he walked to the water's edge. "And I'll keep coming back until I get my goddamn guns!" With a heave, he sent their tent into the river. Back and forth he went, the water carrying off clothes and sandals and Susan's cigar box, Eric's tools flung one at a time before disappearing with a splash. Another kick as Baron nipped his pant cuff. Pain in the beast's whimper.

Susan flinched with the first gunshot. She and Eric cowered behind the boulders, the water up to their chins, a finger-hold grip on the slick stone. Neither peeked as six more shots followed, reverberations that blossomed then faded over the open water. "I will find you!" he cried. "One way or the other, I'll get back what's mine!"

A hail of dirt spit from the cruiser's tires. Susan and Eric waited a minute, then made their way to shore. Their teeth chattered despite the sun. Drying clothes hung in a nearby tree, a pair of shorts and a shirt for each. The van, its tires shot, sat on its rims. Bullet holes in the grill, and in the dirt below, puddles of coolant and oil.

Susan and Eric knelt by Baron's side. Blood soaked the dirt around his gut-spilling belly. Eric sobbed as he used stones and branches to dig a shallow grave, Susan shooing away the flies. Together, they covered him over. She held Eric. A whisper in his ear, a promise they'd be in Florida by week's end.

A bruised sky, lightning in the distance. Susan and Eric stepped across the alfalfa. They'd been on the move since late afternoon, bumming rides and shadowing the tree lines, their eyes nervous with each passing car. Nightfall found them at the edge of her family's fields. In the air, cicadas, the scent of impending rain. The birthright Susan would never inherit whispered with the rustle of leaves and dirt. They crested a gentle slope. A hundred yards downwind, the farmhouse's lit windows strained from the dark.

They sat, Susan leaning into Eric. The earth cool beneath her. Fireflies rising above the leaves. Susan pulled out her cell. She spoke calmly, her anger swallowed back. She would meet Paul in twenty minutes, a public spot on the other side of town. He would get his guns. All Susan wanted in return was his promise to let them go and to bring her mother for a final goodbye.

Five minutes later, Paul and her mother climbed into

his pickup, Paul taking the lane too fast, the headlights bucking, not a flash of his brake lights as he sped onto road. Susan and Eric closed the distance to the farmhouse. The oak leaves shimmied with the first raindrops.

Inside, a quiet that lacked peace. Eric in the pantry, a cardboard box loaded with cereals and bread and crackers, the preserves Susan and her mother had canned. Susan upstairs, ghosts all around—her father, smiling and healthy, the call of his laughter in the narrow hallway. She gathered the clothes she'd passed by before, then to the attic for a box of her father's old things, his size close enough to fit Eric's ropy frame. The key to her car hung from a peg by the back door.

The rain steadier now, the rumble of thunder. The dogs barked. The car started with the second turn of the key, the idle rough but steady. Half a tank—enough to see them across the state line. Gravel crunched beneath her tires. The rain harder, the wipers squeaking. Just past the barn, she shifted into park. She opened the door, Eric's face captured in the sudden light. "What?" he asked.

She ran to the pen. The dogs shadows behind the wire. The gate opened with a wheeze. The friskiest of the bunch knocked Susan back with their headlong dash. She coaxed the lingerers, their collars tugged and their behinds kicked until they scampered after their brothers. Another lightning flash, this one closer, the beasts illuminated as they charged across the open field.

Lucky whimpered, her paw scratching the wire. Susan opened the gate. "Come on, girl."

The dog leapt into the car, its wagging tail thumping between the bucket seats. They drove into the storm, but within an hour, the sky had grown clear. Then stars. Angry messages from Paul on her cell. Susan and Eric talked of Florida, the fruit, the warm, salty breeze. Finally, Lucky fell asleep. In the east, the first hint of dawn.

Beasts and Men

The young man stood in the backyard of the woman who no longer loved him. A single light shone in the kitchen window. The rain that had cut his workday short continued to fall. His hair lay plastered to his skull, and he shivered as the drops trickled down his neck. Hazy mathematics had emptied his wallet, beer and whiskey, snorts of meth in a bar's dingy bathroom. A fight in the parking lot, words he shouldn't have said. His heartbeat thudded in his swollen jaw.

The neighbor's shepherd poked its head from its doghouse. Beneath the man's boots, the squish of flowerbed mud, the blooms gone, winter's lean months near. The meth's dubious chemistry electrified his veins. His machine parts—the sprockets, cogs, and pumps—smoldered, a fire beneath his skin. The shepherd emerged from its house, its ears perked. The man recalled the dog as a pup. "Yes," he'd told the woman he'd loved. "We can get a dog if you'd like."

He ducked beneath the maple's low branches. Tanbark and dead leaves hushed his steps. He stood at the fringe of light that fell from the kitchen window, a spot he'd once ringed with paper lanterns. He saw her face in the colored glow, remembering the warmth of a June night when they'd talked of what might be. A forgotten bucket rested beside the picnic table. Beneath the kitchen window, he turned the bucket over. The leaf-speckled water sloshed around his boots. He stepped onto the bucket and grabbed hold of the ledge. The light shone on his knuckles' dried blood. On the kitchen counter, groceries waiting to be shelved, cut flowers in a vase. Rivulets snaked across the pane, the scene a still-life precisely lit, the once-familiar surroundings blurred by tearing glass and fading memories. The dog he'd bought to please her trotted into the kitchen.

The dog cocked its white-curled head. The tiny thing began to yelp, cries insistent, high-pitched, piercing. The young man placed a hand upon the glass. The vibrations seeped into his palm. The shepherd joined in, barks threatening and deep. Twice, the shepherd choked itself with chain-rattling lunges. Lost in his moment of want and need, the young man howled, too. Here was the chorus of beasts and men.

THE TYCOON

Despondent over the cotton that grew no higher than his shin, the boy's father put a shotgun to his heart and pulled the trigger. The chunks of spine the sheriff pulled from the shanty wall looked like opossum teeth. Surprise! Their crumble-dirt farm swam atop a sea of oil. The first gushing derrick blotted out the sun, and before the roughnecks could cap the flow, the crude lay thick across the land, the puny cotton stalks flattened and drowned. The boy grew into a man. With his millions, he purchased every surrounding farm, not stopping until the horizon was his. Next he bought politicians and sheriffs and everything else that made life bearable in north Texas.

People called him a tycoon. It was his title, the way some people were doctors or pastors. To avenge his father's fate, the tycoon irrigated his clan's original claim, a field of improbable white blooms where rainbows shone in the artificial mist. Beyond this boundary, the bone-dry soil reclaimed the land. The tycoon bought Cadillacs the color of fresh crude. When his dogs rumpled the interior or there weren't enough zeros on the odometer, he gave his cars away. In town, the Sisters of Mercy drove his old Cadillacs; Jimmy Dooley, the one-eyed roughneck, drove one; and so did the waitresses at King's All-Night Truck Stop. The tycoon, now know-ledgeable of the earth and its secrets, imagined the archeologists of the future digging up his old cars. The archeologists would conjure hypotheses about the giant metal husks and their roles in the religious and mating rituals of this forgotten tribe. This made the tycoon smile.

The tycoon adopted strays wherever he roamed. His driveway was a half-mile long, and when he neared his house, he'd slow to a crawl, the car doors flung open. Out rushed his dogs, a slobbering mass of tails and paws. The most agile leapt in, licking his face or lifting their heads to catch the breeze. As the sun set, the tycoon grilled steaks larger than most people's pillows. The dogs waited patiently, knowing their dinner waited when the tycoon had eaten his fill.

At night, the tycoon often returned to the boyhood shack he'd refused to tear down. He picked cotton along the way, careful of the bristles that could draw blood. He rested on the shack's sagging porch and opened the bolls, the soft clumps like four-pointed stars he could cradle in his palm. A dog or two would curl by his side. A tireless oil pump, one of the army that spotted the earth in all directions, labored beside his father's grave. *Shh-thump, shh-thump*, it sang, a lament for the fortune seeker who fell short of his dream; *shh-thump*, a heartbeat that echoed in the tycoon's chest. The tycoon would be buried here someday; his dogs, too. He would return to his father and to the earth. In time, they would all be turned to oil, and with a pump's single heartbeat, they'd be resurrected back onto this land. Or so was his wish.

THE DRESS

The woman hung a dress on the back of her bedroom door. Black dress, white door, and caught in the hazy fringes of sleep, she often believed the dress was floating, a dark fish circling her dreams. The dress was a size six. This was her goal. She dieted. She exercised. At first, she attended meetings, but then she discovered a more intimate communion sitting on her bed and studying the dress.

In summer, she swam in the lake. She could float for hours. The waves undulated beneath her. The lake's shores touched other states, even another country. In the lake, she did not feel large. She floated and swam and floated and swam until the city's buildings and smokestacks dwindled. With the sun warm on her face, she tried to imagine the day she would fit into the dress, but the scene, so deeply wished for, proved difficult to conjure. Instead, she pictured the unseen world beneath her. The menagerie of the forgotten and the lost. Treasures waiting to be washed ashore by the restless tide.

THE CABIN

They'd been on the road for an hour. In another, they'd reach the cabin. They'd cracked the pint once they exited the interstate. Now they followed the river north, two against the current. The leaves gone. The road twisting. The water a gray vein beneath the stars.

Their gear rattled in the pickup's bed. Boots and lanterns. A cooler for beer, another for food. Gas for the generator. Their rifles hung from the rack, and in the cab, the scent of gun oil. They'd first come to the cabin as teens. Twenty years had changed a lot, but not the cabin, not this ride. They passed through river towns. Churches on the squares, white steeples that had seen high water. On the town's shadowed outskirts, smut shops and speakeasies. The river flowed past, its history deep and hidden.

The men passed the pint. Warmth in their bellies, a loosening of muscles. The driver, Kenny, recounted a story fifteen years gone: the two of them saucer-eyed with meth, a traffic stop on this very stretch. The cop with his raised flashlight, a blinding beam. "Every time you told a lie, you twitched," Kenny said. "Like a rusty wind-up toy."

"What the hell were we thinking?"

"You always twitch when you lie. You shuffle or tug your ear or blink. The speed just brought it to another level."

"Really?"

"I know you like a brother." A pause. A doe bolted across the road, a shadow here then gone. "I think Amy's cheating." Amy, his wife. The mother of his sons.

Static on the radio. "You sure?"

"No." They turned off the river road, the flatlands abandoned, an ascent into the hills. "Maybe."

The roadside trees blotted the stars. The road twisted and dipped. A pothole, and the liquor spilled over Kenny's chin. The headlights carved a sliver into the night. The last five miles on unpaved roads. A dirty film on the windshield. A jostling in their bones. The whiskey gone by the time they reached the cabin. Flashlight in hand, Kenny watched his friend crank the generator and turn on the water main. The men put away their food and beer.

Kenny proposed a contest. Forty yards on the makeshift range behind the cabin. The winner would take the next morning's first shot. The target illuminated by the cabin's floodlight and the truck's high beams. An oasis in the dark.

Kenny set the bottle atop a stump near the range's earthen wall. Beneath his feet, mud speckled with shattered glass. Deer tracks, fox. The men counted forty paces. Once they'd left the light, Kenny spoke. "You'd need to tell me if you knew anything."

His friend adjusted the rifle slung over his shoulder. At the count of forty, they stopped. Kenny lifted his barrel and placed his sights on the bottle, the glass a heart of captured light. "I'll go first," he said.

THE STORM

The siren sent the children scrambling into the hallway. They sat as they'd been taught—knees up, bowed heads covered by their hands. The lights flickered and died. In the darkness, a boy cried for his mother. A large window at the hallway's end, a frame for a purple sky veined with lightning. A crack of thunder so loud they cowered beneath its boom. More cries for mothers and fathers. The whispering of prayers. Playground mulch pelted the window, a few specks at first, then steadier, harder. Another flash, the sizzle of split air, the charge felt on the back of every nec k. The wind shrieked, and the pitch escalated until it swallowed the teacher's screams for everyone to stay down. Through the window, they watched the roof of the custodian's shed lift and tumble across the baseball field.

The large boy from the special class at the end of the hallway stood. He shook off the teachers who tried to make him sit. He was like that, mute for the most part, content in his cut-off world until he exploded in fists and tears. The large boy sucked a high-diver's breath and screamed. To the children, he was a silhouette, a figure just a shade darker than the window's midday black. His wail swelled, a coiling that rose from his ribcage and gut, a cry culled from a reservoir of fear the others were only now understanding. The boy howled until he dropped, gasping, to his knees. The hallway window shattered, and in the next second, outside and in changed places.

DESERT MORNING, 1952

The order comes over a crackling loudspeaker, and you crouch into the chill of earth and grave. "This is it!" barks your sergeant. A year has passed since you strangled a man on the Baltimore docks. Cheap whiskey and a marked deck, a scene recalled with a movie-goer's detachment, you the villain, a rendering in gray. The fear of arrest has faded, and in its wake, a new vision of yourself. The spices you once loved now dull upon your tongue. Softness between your legs that night in Reno, the whore's hollow assurance: "Happens to everyone, honey." Dreams of your long-dead mother, her face radiant with heaven's glow, sorrow in her pale eyes.

The loudspeaker: "Sixty seconds." Gaze up, the trench reducing the sky to a cloudless strip. Another desert morning, a light clean and scrubbed, so different from back home.

"Thirty . . . twenty-nine . . ." Your breathing rapid, an equaling of pressure between your gut and head. A white-knuckle grip upon your rifle. The smartasses silent, no more jokes about glowing balls. The private beside you shoves his glasses into his pocket and mutters: "The

Lord is my shepherd . . ." You'd imagined these seconds sagging, but they tick by like all the rest.

"Five . . . four . . ." Put your head over your knees, the way you'd been shown in the training films. The light floods over you. Heat on your neck. Starshine behind your shut eyes. Then the blast, a violence in your bones. The whistling gale of a thousand locomotives. Dirt plunks your helmet, your hunched shoulders.

"Attention!"

Stand and witness the day's second sunrise. The plume lifts, gigantic, terrifying. Beautiful. Another gust, dirt in your mouth and eyes. A whistle blows, and you and a hundred others climb from your trenches.

Walk toward the inferno. The dried sea all around. The plume taller than a mountain and rising still. The man beside you puts on his glasses, the fireball reflected in each lens. A pair of eyes had stared into yours, their light fading. "Forward," the loudspeaker commands. Here and there, wildflowers, colors you hadn't noticed before, delicate blooms trampled beneath your boots. The desert air bakes in your lungs. The man beside you speaks but not to you: "I will fear no evil, for You are with me." You turn once and consider your boots' dusty imprints, testaments to your journey in this valley of death.

No One Owns This Moment But You

A log tumbles into the bonfire's pulsing heart. Sparks fly, an orange swarm released. Shelli's gaze remains heavenward until the last ember dies. She imagines the scene from above, the shine of an earthbound star. Cold tonight. The harvest come and gone. Ahead, the cabin-fever months. Blizzards and drifts. The whine of snowmobiles over the frozen lake. Gutters teethed with icicles.

Shelli's teeth chatter behind her smile. Her bare legs numb beyond pain. The bass drums thud, a second heartbeat in her chest. Firelight on the tubas' golden horns. The park surrounded by fifty-foot oaks, and snared in their skeleton branches, wind-teased ribbons of red and white. The breeze shifts. The smoke swirls over Shelli, the grit in her eyes as she and the other cheerleaders pump their fists. "Roar, Wildcats, ROAR!"

The flames crackle. The heat warps the faces around the fire. The football team with their game jerseys over their sweatshirts. The band in their spangles and fringe. The flag-wavers and baton-twirlers. Beyond them, a crowd double what Shelli had expected, everyone high on football, football, football. Shelli spots Jimmy Nieland, star quarterback of the 2004 squad, slick in his Marine blues, an empty cuff pinned back against his sleeve, his golden arm left mangled in the sand half a world away. Jimmy cups a hand beside his mouth and yells. Never mind the rust on the mill's padlocked gates. Never mind the strip mall's empty stores. There are still heroes to be found.

Shelli and the other cheerleaders pony-step into the space before the bonfire. The blood returns to her wooden legs. Her clapping hands dulled slabs of flesh. She catches sight of her boyfriend through the cheerleaders' choreographed swirl. He stands at the front of the players' pack, his gaze on her alone. The girls shift from a three-deep set into a long line. Shelli's shadow stretches before her. On her command, the group kicks into the Wildcat fight cheer. The words tick from her mouth as thoughtlessly as her steam-puffed breath. A whole, wide swatch of her life has led to this moment, a journey started as a little girl turning cartwheels on soft, summer grass.

The cheer ends, Shelli's body at stiff attention, her head bowed. The crowd answers with a bloody cry. The band kicks in, a cacophony of brass and percussion. The squad huddles for its finale. They speak in voices only they can hear, counting down as Shelli—the squad's smallest girl, its pixie flower—climbs into stirrups of cradled hands.

Up she goes, the earth-abandoning sensation of summer carnival rides. So much is beyond her now. The drumline launches into a furious rat-a-tat-tat. Shelli's thighs quiver until she finds the certainty of balance. With a final lift, the girls raise Shelli high above their heads.

The drumline snaps to a halt. The alma mater's first stanza is hers alone. Her voice rings out, proud, melodic, a ripple she imagines radiating through the park's sudden silence, traveling across town and into the surrounding sea of cut corn. The other cheerleaders join her for the chorus, then the rest of the crowd, but all eyes belong to Shelli. Here, with the fire roaring behind her, she finds another type of balance, her body the fulcrum between light and dark. Cold and warmth. Earth and sky.

Below, her boyfriend, the fire reflected in his watery eyes, and with it, an ambush in Shelli's heart. After the bonfire, she'll tell him she doesn't have to go straight home. She'll ask him to drive down to the old boathouse, and when he reaches beneath her skirt, she won't push his hand away. The backseat will be dark, moonglow on the river.

Shelli sucks in the air, cool and smoky, a last dizzying heartbeat here atop the world. A count of three, a dip and a push, and up she goes, a seated tuck, spread legs parallel to the earth. At her flight's highest point, she touches her toes, a flash of white panties before she begins her fall.

She's practiced this a thousand times, a high diver's discipline, head back, legs straight, toes pointed, her rear gently angled toward the fast-approaching earth. She lies back, accepting it all. She has done her part. She keeps her eyes opened, wanting to remember this night.

THE DRY SEASON

Candice turned from Tom. To her left, a small window, a frame for the bright half moon and starry Atlantic sky. They flew east, into the night. The clock's hands unhinged, a wild spinning of hours. The ocean below, slivers of moonlit swells. Here and there, patches of luminous green, wonders of life and light.

Dim in the cabin. A small screen up front, a romantic comedy, harmless and grating and inexplicably popular. Candice touched the window. Cold glass, her watery reflection. Her father had been an engineer, a man obsessed by how and why and the world's godly order. A story of his: the first jets had sported rectangular windows. Stress on the sharp corners, the fuselage cracking. Spider webs at first, then disaster.

Chuckles in the hushed space. On the screen, a pretty actress in a flowing wedding gown, a barefoot sprint down Fifth Avenue. Candice had not inherited her father's analytic mindset. Motion pictures, jet propulsion, the tensile strength of metals—she could drown in a sea of mysteries. Better to look away and move on.

She wiped spit from Tom's slack lips. He was gone, swallowed by a haze of vodka and Xanax. The trip was a surprise for their fifteenth wedding anniversary. She was touched by the lengths to which he'd gone, his research, the passport he'd secretly procured, an update in his booster shots. In three hours, they'd land in a country she'd read about but never considered. A nation of millions.

Across the aisle, a woman and her sleeping infant. The flight's first hour a shrill protest, a wail choking with hurt and want. A display that had left Candice exhausted and the child's mother near tears. All peaceful now, mother and child a study in bliss. Candice turned back to the window. The sky and sea melted into a single darkness.

A dream of your father standing rink-side. Blood-red scarf around his neck, his scuffed leather coat. You skate to a stop, a shower of ice. Steam from his lips, but not a word. His eyes flitting behind a cloud of white.

Rise from the bed. The room thick despite the air conditioner's rattle. Tug off your sweat-dampened T-shirt. Your pale skin strains against the murky light. You can barely see, yet you're not lost, and the imprint of hundreds of previous hotel rooms guides you through the space's narrow passages. You are a traveler. You pack your suitcases with precision. You gracefully navigate time zones and airport security and subway systems. Years have passed since you've laced up; still you often imagine yourself on the rink, skating forward, beyond friction.

Pull back the curtain. A plane passes, low enough to see silhouettes in the lit windows. The desktop lamp trembles. Think of your own landing, the city a jewel in the dark. The night feels as if it has stretched for days. Soon, the sun will rise. The curtains rustle. A stale resurrection. The scents of other lives.

A buzz from your cell. Grope through your handbag: glasses case, lip balm, a cascade of familiar touches. On the screen, a text from Arthur, your regional manager.

Problems from the other side of the world. A sales-team update on next month's Dallas show. A reminder to download the latest software package.

Tom rolls onto his side. An anniversary trip, a celebration. For him, even more at stake, although he'd never admit it, the chance to revive a fading light. You've had a long run with the thinning demographic of the young and upwardly mobile. A townhouse, new cars, a healthy stock portfolio, your careers progressing more or less as planned, the skater gliding forward. Then your father's murder, bloody, senseless, random. The ice beneath you cracked.

Shut the bathroom door. Another groping. The switch. A burst of light. Your naked, squinting reflection in the mirror. Within a month of burying your father, you endured a series of examinations. The doctor's report— your heart was healthy, your lungs sound, but a vision you'd always possessed was suddenly dead. A simple denial, a disappointment in a world awash in tragedy. Or so you told yourself. Turn the tub's faucet. The pipes hiss. Days will pass before your next shower. Pull the curtain and lift your face to the stream. Let the water beat against your back. A nudge of the hot, then another. This simple luxury is not lost on you this morning. The room fills with steam. Your skin flushes beneath the flow.

Candice and Tom settled into the van's rear. A hard seat, ripped upholstery, duct tape mends. The hotel sidewalk a hive of comings and goings. Africans mostly, dark-skinned men in business suits, some in traditional robes. Arabs, a handful of Europeans. Most texting or holding a phone to their ears. Disjointed conversations. A Babel's Tower echoing beneath the entrance overhang. Taxis and vans lined the curbside. Honking, the pinging idle of four-cylinder engines, the bartering of fares. As Candice and Tom had hunted for their van, a cab backfired, a single pop. Only the tourists failed to duck.

The last of their entourage entered the van. The door slid shut, the window a frame for a slim black man. Chege, their tour guide. Candice had read his story on his website. He was a celebrity of sorts, the winner of a televised talent show. He'd shunned follow-up offers to stay and sing in the capital city. Instead, he started a business, the shuttling of tourists to his village in the bush. Chege and the man he'd introduced as his brother Kwasi secured baggage to the van's roof.

A buzz from Candice's satchel. She retrieved her phone. Another text from Arthur, this one to her alone. A joke about skating in Africa. Arthur enjoyed teasing Candice about her legs, her ability to stand for hours at their convention booths, the knotted calf muscles born from years of balancing atop thin blades. She turned off the phone and returned it to her bag.

The group introduced themselves, English quickly established as a common language. A trick from the business world—Candice's ability to recall names. Each face associated with an initial. The letter leading to a name, and the name leading to a tidbit she'd learned during their introduction. A and B were Annabella and Beatriz, a daughter-mother duo from Argentina. Annabella with the coal-black eyes and bunched mane of wheat hair, a second-year grad student at Duke. Beautiful but easy to imagine as a tomboy, the climber of trees, the swimmer of lakes. Beatriz casually refined, her face etched and sun-hardened. A hollowness in her cheeks, a pastel scarf over her bald head. They spoke of a ranch. The horses they rode over Pampas. A horizon as wide as the sky.

I and M: Ichiko and Minoru, a young couple from Hokkaido. Twin-like with their blunt haircuts and matching cargo shorts and box-fresh hiking boots. Their English hesitant, greetings and innocuous questions. Eager smiles. Awkward silences. They did not hold hands, their connection more subtle, a private harmony of movement and glances.

N was for Neils, a German giant. His wide-brimmed hat scraped the van's ceiling. His rounded middle more thick than fat, a school teacher from Bavaria. Fair skinned. Circular glasses he was fond of cleaning, thinning blond hair. His shirt's armpits already circled with sweat. "Sorry, sorry," he said, his elbow poking Ichiko as he fumbled through his camera case. He offered a bow. "Very sorry, my friend."

Ichiko bowed in return. "Mine is the pleasure."

Kwasi pulled from the curb. Chege reached back and locked the side door. "In the city, a good idea." They had yet to escape the hotel's drive. A woman in a maid's blue dress called Chege's name. She said more, a language already pleasant to Candice's ear, shimmering, a ripe music. Chege smiled, an invitation of yellow teeth. Kwasi turned, his English less practiced: "'Chege, sing for me,' she says."

The light changed. They merged into the sluggish maw. More horns, radios blaring from open windows. Five minutes to crawl one kilometer. The heat built, the windows up and the air conditioning weak. Five minutes of pickup trucks with dubiously secured cargo. Pirate taxis. Motor scooter daredevils. On the sidewalk, vendors and their carts, a pack of blue-skirted schoolgirls who beat the van to every corner. A slam of breaks, and Candice and the others lurched forward. Five minutes, and already Candice appreciated a different energy here, a heartbeat desperate and chaotic and infectious.

Neils snapped the journey's first picture. Curbside, a car with a raised hood, smoke billowing from the engine. A bike taxi passed, the driver without shoes and shirt, a man in a sharp business suit in the back. The snarl intensified, a commotion at the intersection ahead. They pulled alongside another van, a vehicle similar in make and model. In it, a crush of bodies, women mostly, the seats filled, more perched upon their laps. A woman in the last seat turned toward Candice. She was attractive, her eyes young yet weary. She wore a sleeveless dress, a scarf over her head. She didn't wince when the heavy woman shifted upon her lap. In Candice's thoughts, an appreciation of alternate fates. Chege's van lurched ahead.

There was a time, early in her traveling life, when the weight of strangers had consumed Candice. Amid the bustle of streets and terminals, she studied those around her, her spirits buoyed by a long-shot's hope, logic trumped by the belief that within the crowds there must be a familiar face. A high school friend. A sorority sister. A skater from the old circuit. Of course she understood the odds, yet these yearnings remained stubborn until the morning she found herself captured in a shoulder-to-shoulder throng on a Manhattan street corner. She could move neither forward nor back, her view of sky and buildings hemmed in by the men who towered above her. The crowd pressed forward, a surge of bodies, Candice carried along even though her feet had been lifted from the sidewalk. Claustrophobia, a suffocation rooted deep beneath her skin. The herd crossed the street, and she fought to the front. Relief, a bit of open air, and in the moment, she surrendered her yearnings for recognition and immersed herself in the river of similar molecules, the daisy chains of carbons and amino acids, the chorus of heartbeats and constricted bowels. Here, in anonymity, waited a deeper communion than any haphazard reunion could bring.

Their van reached the intersection. A policeman in blue tooted his whistle, his white-gloved hands orchestrating the traffic's flow. An overturned cart blocked the road. Potatoes and green beans littered the macadam. A donkey on its side, a man kneeling close, his face in his hands. Two more policemen tied a rope around the donkey's neck and struggled to drag the beast to the curb.

Downtown's tall buildings faded into apartments and shops. Open-air markets lined with vendors and their stalls. A clutch of factories. A wide scrub field, trash mounds, tires, picked-over cars. Birds circled overhead, and a stench invaded the van. Cell phone towers strained to the clouds. Then a stretch of corrugated tin roofs, a few at first, then many. The roofs reflected dull glints of sun, a rising and falling like crests on a frozen sea. Ashy smoke columns bled into the wide, blue sky.

"Shantytown," Chege said. "Very bad place."

Neils and Minoru took pictures. The shantytown's hovels stretched across the field. If Candice looked straight, the shacks blurred into a single squalor, but a perpendicular view brought frozen moments, sagging clothes lines, ghost children between flickering veils of metal and smoke. Kwasi fiddled with the radio tuner. The huts thinned then disappeared.

In time, the road narrows to two lanes. The windows down. Your hair whips, words dulled by seashell acoustics and the engine's whine. The wind a baking current. A new scent here, open, dusty. Here is the Africa you envisioned. Flatlands of brown and green. Sparse, squat trees. Above, the crystalline blue of the dry season.

Kilometers pass without a hut or car. The macadam gives way to packed dirt, and the vibrations invade your bones. No one speaks. You think of the predawn rides with your father, rinks up and down the coast. Steam from his thermos. The long silences you never minded. His hands steady on the wheel.

On the shoulder, a fallen steer. Bloat in its belly, and the swell lifts its back hoof skyward. You sit back, accepting the fragile security of the van and the unforgiving landscape all around. What happens now is beyond you. It's an echo of how you feel on every takeoff, that first angled view of the receding earth and the swallowing back of panicked instincts that date back to a place like this, the cradle of your kind. Surrender, and with it comes a shift in perspective, a fatalistic calm.

Sharp words from the front seats. Chege cranks his window and gestures to his brother. You spot the car, its hood raised. A shirtless man stands in the middle of the road. His hands wave, a wild plea. Kwasi stomps the gas. The man doesn't move. A week before you left, you received the embassy's letter detailing the rise of lawlessness in the bush, the khat-chewing highwaymen and the ransoms they demand. Kwasi lays a hand on the horn but doesn't lift his foot. The man steps aside at the last second. He shakes his fist before he's swallowed by a swirl of dust.

Chege turned. "The village."

Ahead, a collection of huts, a few trees. At the village's center, a larger building of smooth, white stone, an open-aired crown at its top, a belfry without a bell. Candice had seen the pictures on Chege's website. She'd read the tense-challenged narrative of the building's history, its start as a mission in the late 1800s, the property in disrepair until Chege brought home his TV winnings. An ox shuffled along the roadside. The man behind the ox tapped a switch against the beast's flank. Kwasi beeped. The man lifted his switch in greeting.

A crumbling wall, its stone matching the mission's white, surrounded the village. Inside, tiny huts, boxes with roofs of tin and thatch. The sputter of the van's muffler echoed off mud walls. Two women carried water jugs atop their heads. A pack of children drew to the road's edge, their soccer game abandoned. They wore western shorts and T-shirts, most barefoot. Chege leaned from the window, beckoning and calling. The children gave chase. The tallest boy was also the swiftest. For a few strides, he managed to run alongside the van, his palm pressed against Candice's window. Her hand lifted from her lap, an instinctual urge to return his touch. The van rolled ahead. The boy, unable to keep pace, receded in its wake.

A wide courtyard sat in front of the mission. In its center, a boarded-up well. Kwasi circled the courtyard, a maneuver that allowed the children to catch up. The dust settled into a knee-high haze, the children moving through a scene culled from Hollywood's interpretations of dreams. The van stopped in front of the mission steps. The children massed by the doors, yelling, an offering of upturned palms. Chege produced a bag of penny candy, and he and Kwasi handed out the treats. The bright wrappers crinkled and fell to the ground.

Candice and the others climbed from the van. Kinks in her muscles. Neils produced a red bandana and mopped the sweat from his face. Chege, his hands clasped, returned the bows of Ichiko and Minoru. Kwasi untied the ropes that secured the rooftop's luggage. The children pressed toward the visitors, their cheeks balled with candy, the glint of sugar in their eyes. The braver ones stepped forward. Annabella knelt and allowed a girl to examine her feather earrings. A boy laid a hand on Candice's arm, his palm soft and cool.

An older boy exited the mission. "Jomo," Kwasi called, gesturing toward the bags he'd set in the courtyard. Jomo stood taller than the other children, matchstick legs, a long, thin neck, a serious expression. He did not join the others in their begging or curious touching. His shoulders slumped as he lifted a pair of bags. Chege rubbed the boy's head as they passed on the mission steps.

A rooster pecked around the boarded-up well. In the shadow of a hut's overhang, three old men played cards at a folding table. A woman carried a laundry basket filled with white sheets. They turned for a moment, but their gazes did not linger. Candice imagined how she and the others appeared to the locals. Exotic. Wealthy. The sons and daughters of powerful nations. The men returned to their cards. The woman readjusted her grip upon the basket and walked on. The adults understood what the children did not: that a traveler was a breeze, a brushing moment against the skin, here and gone. The traveler was the shadow, not the tree. The traveler had abandoned his home, and with it, the physical scaffoldings of his days. He had willingly cast himself into the realm of strangers. He was left only with an itinerary of sights to see and the freedom of unclaimed hours, a series of voids in which he was free to either lose or redefine himself.

"Please, do not give them anything," Chege said. He waved his hands, attempting to shoo the children but only succeeding in drawing them closer. "If you do, they will not leave you alone."

The children tugged his shirt. Some chanted his name, hands outstretched. The tall, fast boy reached into Chege's shirt pocket. Jomo returned. He chided the children, a tone harsher than Chege's. When they didn't retreat, he ripped the soccer ball from one boy's grip. He kicked the ball, a high, arcing flight, a thump at the courtyard's far end. The children ran, a jostling stampede through the dust. Jomo wrestled two more bags across the mission's threshold.

A man in a long robe appeared at the mission's side. In one hand, a frayed rope, its end looped around a small goat's neck. In his other hand, a knife as long as his forearm. An argument between the man and Kwasi, voices raised, the goat bleating. The robed man waved his hand. The sun glinted along the blade. He turned, the rope tugged hard. A bell around the goat's neck, jagged, coppery notes.

Chege paused at the top of the mission steps. "Welcome to my home. To my village." Jomo, laden with another round of bags, squeezed past. "I was one of these children you see. So were my sons, one who lives back in the city, another at the university. Their education and this mission paid for by good fortune and my voice." He placed his palm flat against his chest, lifted his chin, and sang a bird-like song. Candice and the others clapped. Chege offered a theatrical bow.

"And today, my heart sings, too, because I can share this with you, my new friends. Tonight we will have a humble feast, but we have made good time." He checked his watch. The goat bleated. "We have five hours or so. Your rooms are waiting. Water and fruit are there for you. You may rest, or if you would like, I will show you the mission and the village." His smile wilted. His voice lowered, a tone of warning. "But it is very important that you do not leave without one of us as your guide. Please understand how important this is, no?"

He stepped aside and gestured toward the mission's shadowed interior. "Please, come in."

Late afternoon sun slants into the room. You lie naked on a narrow mattress. Around you, a delicate scrim of mosquito netting. Tom drifts, a crinkled smile, a satisfied sleep. You didn't come, yet you don't mind; your desire not for fulfillment but connection, a taste of grounding in this odd land.

Brush the hair from his forehead. Yours was a dormitory romance. Tom a late-bloomer in a suddenly grownup body, you behind in calculus as you readied for a regional meet, your focus heaped on a soon-to-die dream. A knock on his door, an asking for help. His eyes gleamed as he explained quadratic derivatives. Nirvana on the stereo. He liked you, yes, but his excitement was also piqued by his passion for the theoretical, the invisible genius he still believes exists in this world. Outside the subject of math, you thought him shy. Then you grew to understand he was simply the possessor of deeply engrained manners and an acute sense of fair play, his outward reserve a mask for a heart keen to rush forward. His eyes dampened in darkened movie theaters. His wallet opened when charities called. His gift a sincere yearning to believe the best in everyone. Almost twenty years together, and you can count on one hand the number of times he's raised his voice.

His lips sputter, and the first jagged snores rise from his throat. You shrug into his shirt, his scent near. Slide into your boots, mindful of Chege's warnings of scorpions. The children's soccer game rages in the courtyard. The clanking of pots calls from the kitchen. The goat no longer bleats. Your room is one of two upstairs. "The priest's chambers," Chege said.

The boots' untied laces whisper over the floorboards. A drop of come falls from between your legs. You crouch and wipe the spot, the glob cool on your fingers. The floorboards are rutted and scuffed, and you imagine the room's history of secrets, its confessions and bartered deals. A washbowl and pitcher sit atop the dresser. Slip your hands into the bowl, and when you lift them, a droplet shower, ripples on the surface. Rub your hands over your face and neck, once, then again, your cheeks dried with a rough towel. You're accustomed to strange beds, yet you've never stayed in a room like this. In a few days you will leave this country. A memory: your father's thumbnail over your skates' blades, a testing of sharpness, a shaving thin and translucent. A memory of you will remain in this room, a snapshot never to grow old. When you pull the hairbrush from your bag, your cell phone tumbles to the floor.

Consider the blank screen. You're miles from a signal. Walk across the room, your hair brushed in long, repetitive strokes. You think of Arthur and Dallas, a convention center like a dozen others, muted echoes beneath a high, girder-crossed ceiling. You'll stand for hours, discussing product and market, and Arthur will joke about your legs, your stamina. Later, dinner with clients, drinks in a dim bar. Men will act like the frat boys they once were. Flirting at different levels, the schmoozing of commerce, Arthur's groping hand beneath the table. This past year, he's become your sometimes-lover. Yes in Toronto the week before Thanksgiving; no last month in Memphis. Arthur is easy, uncomplicated, vain, the kind of man who's carried the jockish ethos of his teens into adulthood. He divides his world into neat categories—players and spectators, winners and losers. He is accustomed to getting his way, but you decide when and how, his yearnings as shallow as they are predictable; your trysts dictated by your words, your whims. Your body.

Tom rolls onto his side, mutters a few syllables, and resumes his snoring. The sun falls upon the mosquito net, a tomb of captured light. He, too, has lost a vision of himself. You've rarely discussed the matter, but in the past year, you've come to know the hush of vacant rooms, and the silence's depth unnerves you. Robbed of words, you're left with grand gestures. Tom has reached out, this trip, an adventure to be shared. You've spread your legs for another man, a betrayal, if discovered, certain to break Tom's heart.

Voices from outside, the calls of children at play. You stand by the window. Smoke on the breeze. The children sprint across the courtyard dirt. The pecking chickens scatter. A boy kicks the ball back to the scrum, the game rejoined. Chege and Jomo carry a wooden table down the mission steps and set it alongside another in the building's shadows.

Run a finger over the ledge's dust. A new scent meshes with the fire's smoke, the flavor of burning meat. In the dirt alongside the table, a length of rope.

The breeze picked up after sundown, a coolness that seemed impossible that afternoon. Stars, more than Candice had ever seen, single glints, hazy clusters. The cook's fire reduced to embers. A pair of carbine lanterns on the table. An oily scent, a flickering glow.

In the courtyard, Neils and Annabella played soccer with two children unclaimed by the hour. Annabella skilled, feints and jukes that had the rest stumbling. She flipped the ball up, and the children counted the juggling kicks that kept it aloft. Neils surprised Candice with his deft passes, a header all agreed was the night's most beautiful goal. Empty plates on the table, glasses Chege topped with another round of potent, bitter wine. Candice sated and buzzed. The goat's meat in her belly, and she felt stronger for it.

The soccer game ended. Annabella and Neils returned to the table, the children in their wake. Candice sat on the bench's end. The smaller boy stood by her. The white of his eyes shone in the pulsing light. He reached out and brushed the tips of her hair. Chege called the children then addressed his guests: "They are thieves. Check your pockets."

Jomo leaned between Candice and Tom and lifted their plates. The stack rattled in his grip. He passed the cook on the kitchen stoop. The cook showed little interest in the proceedings, his duties ending when the meal was served. Now he relaxed, and the tip of his rolled cigarette glowed when he brought its wet end to his lips. One of the children found the goat's bell. He rang it, a series of loud clanks. A dog's bark answered from the night.

Neils set down his wine. Glare on his glasses, his eyes masked. He pointed to Candice and Tom. "We have North Americans." His finger drifted to Annabella and Beatriz. "South Americans." He poked his chest and gestured to the others. "A European, Asians, and Africans." He took a sip of wine. "Now where's that Australian we ordered?"

"Run off with the Eskimo, I imagine," Beatriz said. "Wait, that's not Antarctica, is it?"

"No one lives in Antarctica," Annabella said. "Explorers, filmmakers, but not permanently. At least I believe."

Candice rubbed Tom's shoulder. She felt liberated, unburdened and at peace. This morning, she'd met these people as strangers on a hotel sidewalk. Now they were comrades, fellow adventurers, their fates united for the next two days. "Antarctica is next on our travel list."

"Really?" Neils asked.

"No," Candice said. They all laughed.

More wine, a desert cake thick with nuts and raisins. Conversation, and Candice sank back, content in her silence, her understanding of the others growing. She wondered if Neils was one those big men never quite comfortable in his skin, his conversation peppered with apologies for the nudgings of his elbows and feet. A gold band on his finger, a story of a son who loved trains and a wife who limited her travel to resorts and hotels. Ichiko and Minoru struggled to share the framework of their lives. Minoru a government official at the city docks, an inspector of freight. Ichiko even less versed, her duties as a nurse half spoken, half mimed. Her hand held a phantom syringe. Chege by her side, his sleeve rolled up, wincing as he received the injection. Annabella so pretty, a more mature beauty waiting. She, like Candice, was a listener, her conversation polite, complementary. She filled her mother's water glass, drew the shawl over her shoulders as the chill built. Beatriz the most animated, her English accented but unflagging. Her bits of German a sidelight that Neils greeted with hearty laughter, yet beneath, glimmers of pain. Labored swallows. IV pockmarks on the cup-holding hand she raised to her lips. Fluidity invaded Candice's thoughts, a confusion of perspective, the inability to determine if the moment was dreamy or hyper real. Chege laid a map across the table. The map's colors had faded at its fold lines, its edges rustling until Chege anchored the paper with lanterns and wine glasses.

"We are here," Chege said. The village a dot on an arrow-straight road. Only now did Candice notice the index finger that ended before the last knuckle. The breeze stiffened. The map's unmoored corner slapped the lantern's base. Candice, her skin still warm from the day, shivered. A sudden exhaustion in her bones. The stubby finger veered to the northwest, a patch of tan, a space unclaimed.

"Twenty-five kilometers," Chege said. The finger rested on a glob of blue.

Candice couldn't budge her gaze from the amputated finger. She thought of histories, cruel and not. She thought of the experiences beyond language. She leaned against Tom.

"A lake," Chege said. "But in the dry season little more than a watering hole."

His finger traced other paths, migration routes, herds driven by ancient instincts. He guaranteed nothing. "The land's rhythm is not mine." He smiled, and Candice, the hardened traveler, gave over to her host's kindness, his sincerity. "I can only listen to it, and for that, I am thankful." He cupped his hands around the lake, his palms a bowl of tan flesh. "I bring my guests here to see the most beautiful thing I know. This makes me very happy."

The boy who'd touched Candice's hair crept from the shadows. Candice alone noticed him, the others intent on the map and Chege's words. The boy moved forward, cautious, determined, his bare feet silent across the dirt. His eyes flitted between Candice and the pushed-aside plates at the table's edge. He snatched a cube of goat cheese and shoved it in his mouth.

Kwasi leapt to his feet. He ran after the boy, shouting. The boy juked, the table and the tourists used as a barrier, Kwasi's advances met with nimble retreats. Chege laughed, encouraging the boy. The chase looped around the mission, a disappearance into the shadows before returning to the table. The boy brushed past Candice, snatched another cheese cube, and sprinted into the night. Kwasi shambled to a stop. He pressed his hands into his knees, his sides heaving.

A lull settled over the courtyard. The last sips of wine waited in their glasses. Neils produced a crumpled cigarette pack. "The remnants of a regrettable habit," he explained, a single smoke his reward for reaching another day's end. He offered the pack to the others, but only Kwasi accepted. The flick of a lighter, two faces illuminated. The scent of tobacco joined the fire's smoldering embers. Kwasi handed his cigarette to Jomo. The boy held the filter with a hard pinch, his dry cough suppressed as he handed the cigarette back.

"There is a song my people sing the night before a hunt," Chege said. "My grandfather sang it, as did his grandfather, back to the time this mission was built and farther back still." He cleared his throat. His thin chest swelled. Silence at the table. The tonalities and rhythms were unfamiliar to Candice's western ear, the words a mystery, yet the song's tide of strength resonated, its communion between man and this wild place. Smoke rose from Neils's cigarette, and Candice imagined Chege's voice following the same path, the lovely notes rising to the all and everything of the stars.

You wake to a timid rapping. Jomo's voice from the other side of the door: "Awake, OK?" Another knock. "Awake, man and lady, OK?"

Rub your eyes. The courtyard rooster crows. The faintest of lights. Tom dresses and checks the single bag you'll take to the campsite. You pour water into the basin. Cup your hands and take a drink, another handful splashed over your face. In your temples, the squish of too much wine. Tom joins you, a joke about anticipation, your reflections in the dull mirror.

Pause by the window. Voices from the courtyard, Chege and Kwasi and Neils. A two-wheeled trailer now hitched to the van, a rectangle of wood, a perimeter of metal railings. A backpack slung over your shoulder, you exit the mission and cross from shadows to sun, chill to warmth. Your muscles stir. The strutting rooster pauses and crows. Shield your eyes. Above, a blue-sky ocean, ships of puffy clouds.

Small birds light from the belfry. Chege, his arms filled with camping gear, bids good morning.

The others in your party gather around the tables. They are subdued, polite, their skin pale in the morning sun. The cook brings plates of figs and warmed flatbread. Jomo pours coffee into chipped cups. A rusted pickup passes, a pair of young men holding tight in the bed. In the mission's shadows, the boy Kwasi chased last evening. The boy doesn't bother you this morning, his attention on a stick he holds, pictures sketched in the courtyard dirt.

Jomo sets a load of bedrolls into the trailer. On Chege's shoulder, a rifle from a distant war, bolt action, a stock of worn wood. The cook sweeps the mission's front steps. You cross the courtyard, a last chance to use the outhouse. Close the door and hold your breath. Slits of light fall from a high window. Swat back the flies, your gut twisting with the morning's coffee and last night's dinner. Once you were a skater, a childhood dedicated to the human expression of precision. At your best, you flirted with mastery. Toe loops, axels, camels—your father preached the divinity of practice. *Mechanics first*, he said, *and the rest will follow*. Him on his skates, the physical tools never his, but his heart! His heart! If you trembled before a competition, you locked yourself in a stall and stuck a finger down your throat. The convulsions cleansed you, a solitary violence, a confirmation that will trumped flesh. Zip up, and once outside, you draw a deep breath. Warmer still, the promise of heat. Your emaciated shadow stretches across the dirt.

You wait outside the van. Neils and Minoru fiddle with their cameras. Jomo hands each tourist a canteen, tins dented and wrapped in canvas. Sip, a metallic shimmer on your tongue. "There are no wells once we leave the village," Chege said last night. "In the dry country, water is as important as blood."

Chege supervises the trailer's final preparations. Tents

and a field stove. Three of the four corners anchored by large coolers. You slather on sun block. Jomo, a shovel in one hand and a machete in the other, stares as he passes. Chege slides back the van's door. "Come, please."

Habit dictates your return to the back seat. Kwasi starts the van. A dog pokes its head from a hut and barks. Jomo settles into the corner of the trailer unclaimed by a cooler and gathers the bedrolls to his side. Chege secures a rope around the boy's chest with a series of loops and knots. Back home, you'd refuse to let the van start. You'd call the police. But you're not home, and you can't deny the rhythms that radiate from the sky and soil and their warning that your way is not wanted here.

The trailer shimmies as the van circles the courtyard. The boy with the stick fades into the swirling dirt. The cook pauses in his sweeping and waves goodbye. The van picks up speed. The village's huts fade. The packed gear trembles. Jomo's grip tightens on the trailer's sides.

The sun climbs. Captured flies thump against the windows. The road straight and unpaved. Forty minutes, Chege said. Inside the van, polite conversation then silence. The heat builds. All eyes lost in the scenery, a flatland of dirt and grass the color of dirt. Here and there, a tree, gnarled trunks, green canopies flattened by the wide sky. Glacier-peaked mountains in the distance. Colors you know, but also different, hues warped by latitude and the bone-dry air.

Minoru speaks to his wife. Ichiko ducks and looks out her window. Twenty meters from the road, a circling of vultures, ugly, bald-headed birds, wings spread, their cautious turns echoed by the flock above, a spiraling dance ending as the birds disappear into the tall grass.

"The cycle of life," Neils says. He slides the cap back onto his lens. "This is what we came to see, no?"

A bump in the road. Water spills from the canteen raised to your lips. Wetness on your lap. You turn. Jomo pushes aside the bedrolls that have tumbled onto his legs.

"There," Chege says. He points to a gentle ridge, a crest of thirty-some meters rising from the flatlands.

Kwasi turns the wheel, and the van veers from the road. The tall grasses hiss against the van's sides. Birds scatter, frantic wing flaps like a host of tiny explosions. Jomo clutches the trailer's sides, a smile on his face.

The ridge grows as you approach, a rising crest of dirt and rock. The van rolls to a stop at the hill's base, a grassless spot, a handful of trees. The dust swirls behind you, Jomo with a hand covering his mouth. In the clearing, a ring of stones.

Step from the van, your boots upon the dirt, a feel so different than macadam. The sun beats down. Chege chambers a round into the rifle. The bolt clicks, a single, sharp note. Jomo wriggles free from the rope's bindings. Chege approaches you, but then pauses. Tremors beneath your feet. You reach for Tom's arm. Not an earthquake, these vibrations tamer, more persistent, steadily growing. Chege smiles. "You feel it, yes. Now see."

Chege slides the rifle's strap over his shoulder. "There," he says, pointing to a lone thorn tree atop the ridge. He leads the way, the slope—steeper than you expected—speckled with rocks and clinging weeds. The rust-red dirt gives way with each step, thin cascades, a dozen tiny slips, your shadows shortening as you climb. Halfway up, you glance back. A parched breeze touches your face. Kwasi unloads the first tent. Jomo rights the fire ring's stones. Within the ring, a charred circle, the black speckled by white moths. Jomo shushes them, a wave of thin fingers. The moths flutter off.

Chege is the first to reach the top. In his blue shirt, he belongs to the stretching sky. You and Tom join him. The air here does little to ease your stirred pulse. Ichiko and Minoru close behind, Neils visibly fatigued. Beatriz pauses before the final push, Annabella offering her canteen.

Chege waves his hand, a gesture that sweeps over the valley. "This is why we come."

The valley opens before you. The lake, perhaps one hundred by two hundred meters, dominates the near distance. Sloping shores lead to the water, land submerged in the rainy season. Beyond the lake, grasslands, and upon them, a moving shadow, a pulse like a wave cut loose from the ocean.

"Wildebeests," Chege says.

Tom offers the binoculars, but you feel an obligation to witness the spectacle in its entirety, to honor the landscape's grand scale. The first of the wildebeests reaches the shore, its great, horned head lowered, an action echoed as hundreds of others press to the water's edge.

Minoru and Neils erect their tripods and twist on their telescopic lenses. Before the trip, Tom bought a new camera, modest in comparison, the piece held to his eye as he adjusts the focus. Jomo lugs shade umbrellas to the ridge. Chege plunges the wooden tips into the earth, the shafts twisted until the umbrellas stand more or less at attention. Jomo kneels below, the bases shored with piles of rocks and dirt. With a push, the tops spring open, a blossoming of faded canvas.

An elephant herd has claimed the shore opposite the wildebeests. Calves huddle beside the adults. A tusked bull raises his trunk, a showered mist, water droplets prismed in the unbothered sunlight. Cranes fly in from the south. The birds' landings tear scars into the water's tranquil surface, long ripples in their wake.

The hours pass. Pictures are snapped, wildly at first, the clicks insistent then settling. You take a turn with Neil's massive binoculars, a vision with the power to place you among the beasts, the eyes and manes and hides only waiting for your touch. In the sloped dirt before you, a half-buried ribcage. Beneath the bleached-white bones, a spider web, a delicate weaving, a faint glimmer in the sun.

"I am happy," Chege says. He sits, his forearms resting on bent knees. "There is much to see today. Maybe the wildebeests again tomorrow. Perhaps zebras. All coming and going. Only the cats and crocodiles staying." He looks to the sky. "I would come here as a boy with my father, just as he'd come with his father." His waving hand indicates the passing of generations. "Then I made my money with something as silly as my voice, a plaything. They said, 'Chege, make a record. Chege, sing in my club.'" He shakes his head. "No, I said. All I wanted was to show people this. People from all over the world. I wanted to share this place."

Bring the binoculars back to your eyes. An elephant's great flapping ears. Dirt crusted in its wrinkled skin. Then a burst of activity, an excitement mirrored on the ridge top. Chege points. A wild clicking of cameras. Commotion at the water's edge. A crocodile has clamped onto an antelope calf's leg. Water splashes. The animals on the shore shrink back. Another snap of jaws and the flailing ends. The crocodile pulls back, the calf taken, a last glimpse of its head, then gone.

The sun sinks. Your shadows stretch into the valley. In you, a churning you hadn't expected. You feel as if you are gazing backwards in time. You feel the pull of earth and water. Gradually, the lake's tides become your own, the heat and dust belonging to you as much as they do to the beasts. The themes of their dance make themselves evident. The push of life, silent, inexorable. The vulnerability of the young and the old. The driving of hunger and thirst. You feel connected. Humbled. Awed. You stay until the light begins to bleed from the sky. Jomo calls from below. The fire burns. "Eat!" he yells. His voice thinned by the opened space. "Eat time, all of you!"

The breeze picked up at twilight. The tents' canvas skins rippled. Jomo crouched by the fire. They'd brought kindling and logs. The flames crackled. Jomo looked up, called to Chege. Chege lifted his gaze to the darkening sky. The geese approached in a great cloud.

Their honking calls deafening as they disappeared over the ridge. Chege smiled. "This is good. Tomorrow you will see."

The stars appeared. Jomo fed another log into the fire. The boy had worked since sunrise, a crime back home, but here, a privilege, his labors earning enough to pay for a bag of flour, a pocket knife, a new pair of shoes. The flames grew. Sparks lifted, a short-lived dance. Candice imagined the eyes that studied them, the animals crouched in the night.

They sat around the fire, a circle of folding chairs and stools and coolers. They ate bread and fruit, strips of goat meat that had been packed in the cooler and then warmed over the flames. Candice sipped wine from a tin cup, the bite welcome in her throat, a shiver inside to match the one on her skin. Chege sat, rifle by his side, eating only after Candice and the others had finished.

Neils was the first to retrieve his camera. The others did the same and pulled their chairs and stools close. Jomo held a handful of twisted grasses over the flames. The grass caught, a crackling torch, a moment of illumination before he dropped the bundle into the ring of stones. The tourists accessed their memory cards. Back they went, a reversal of time, the view from the ridge, the ride, the village, last night's dinner, the city's traffic. Then a few more clicks, the places from which they'd come. Jomo drew close, interested in a way he hadn't been before. Ichiko and Minoru showed their garden, slate paths and delicate plants, a wooden arch, a bench for two. Beatriz introduced them to Annabella's brothers and sisters, handsome children, their eyes bright, health in their wide smiles. Then a picture of Annabella's boyfriend. Annabella blushed. Jomo pointed to the screen. "Annabella's man," he said, kissing the smoky air.

"Yes, Jomo." Beatriz smiled. "I'm afraid it's love."

Neils shared images of his wife, demure and blond, a piano teacher. He spoke of a parade of students from noon to supper, the tick of a metronome, sour notes. A shot of his son, a lanky boy, a frame ready to sprout. "Your age," he said to Jomo.

Jomo moved to Tom and Candice. He gestured to their camera. "Home?"

"Sorry," Tom said. "New camera. New card." He clicked back to the first picture he'd taken. Candice on the plane, the small window a halo behind her head. The boy returned to the fire. He sat before the flames, back turned.

Another round of wine. Ichiko declined, a smile between her and her husband, then the confession of her pregnancy. A wave of congratulations, handshakes. Beatriz embraced Ichiko, the older woman apologizing for her tears. Jomo stood nearby, perplexed, until Chege translated. The boy smiled, clapped.

Another log for the fire. The breeze whistled in the thorn trees. Candice listened for cries from the other side of the ridge but heard none. The wine mellowed her thoughts. Neils smoked his nightly cigarette, another given to Kwasi, the last puffs saved for Jomo. Chege started the van, the engine's rattle foreign in the hushed night. The headlights shone across the clearing. Shovel in hand, Kwasi ventured to the fringe of light and dark, a shadow in the empty landscape. The shovel bit into the earth.

Chege handed each woman a wad of toilet paper. In the near distance, another shush of metal and dirt. "Many predators here. It is important to cover our scents." He shouldered the rifle, and Candice noticed the only time he didn't smile was when he was handling the gun. His worn boot scraped the earth. "Kick the dirt back when you are done."

Kwasi returned. He shut off the headlights, but kept the engine and parking lights on. Jomo climbed into the driver's seat. The boy fiddled with the radio, the knob twisted, static until he found a weak-signaled station.

Rifle in hand, Chege led the women from camp. He pointed out the holes, random craters no more than three meters apart. He walked ahead, his back to them, and faded into the dark.

For a moment, the women didn't move. Beatriz was the first to unzip. "When in Rome," she said. She crouched over a hole. The hiss of urine gurgled in the dry earth. "I've never been a fan of clichés, but this one, I understand."

Ichiko was next, then Annabella and Candice. From the van came the radio's faint strains. Candice was the first to move her bowels, and with it, both she and Beatriz crumbled into a giggling fit, the laughter finding all the women, feeding upon itself with every subsequent call. When they were done, they covered the holes as they'd been told, Candice's boot delivering a final tamp for good measure.

The men followed, the women by the campfire. Flashlight in hand, Kwasi entered each tent, a final search for scorpions, the tents' sides lit and shadow-cast. Jomo brought the women a bowl of water. "For washing," he said. Candice took the scarf from her neck and dipped it in the bowl. The cloth cool against her face, a rinsing of the day's grit.

The men returned. Chege led them to their tents. Candice had been trying to figure the sleeping arrangements, and only now did she realize her hosts would sleep under the stars. "Goodnight, my friends," Chege called. "Sleep well."

Tom secured the tent flap. A musty scent rose from the bedrolls. Candice held a flashlight while Tom opened the sleeping bags. From outside, the sound of a flute, tender, bare notes. She and Tom knelt and gazed out the mended screen atop the flap. Chege and Kwasi lit by the flames, the boy sitting nearby. Kwasi held his pursed lips against a wooden flute. Chege sang, a different song tonight, his voice smaller, more brittle, a begging invitation to be counted as part of all the living things they were about to lie among.

Candice pulled herself close to Tom. The day's weariness came in a sudden wave. She surrendered to its weight. Soon she was gone.

You wake early. Gray light eases through the flap's screen. Outside, the stirrings of morning camp, a hushed conversation between Chege and Kwasi. The rattle of pots. The first, smoldering scent of kindling. Tom sleeps. The smell of your bodies has massed beneath the tent's shell, a scent sour yet not unpleasant. You lay a hand on Tom's chest and allow your thoughts to drift.

Jomo screams. A spasm seizes Tom's body, his eyes blinking. The boy screams again, a single word repeated, then a call for Chege. Tom fumbles into his shorts and boots. In his eyes, an uncertainty of place, the ashen expression of a man struggling with the boundary of dreams and reality. He pulls back the tent flap and tells you to stay behind.

You sit in the dim tent. More voices, the boot falls of running feet, the boy still yelling. You dress and step outside.

Cooler here, the shadows deep, the sky colored by the sunrise that has yet to crest the ridge. Chege dashes past, a machete in one hand, a hacked branch in the other. He joins Kwasi and Jomo and kneels near the van. Behind them, Tom and the other bleary tourists.

"A cobra," Tom says.

"The heat calls them," Chege says. He jabs the branch beneath the van. "The engine warm from last night."

You kneel. The cobra lies coiled in the shadows beneath the van. The snake sways, head raised, hood flared. Chege thrusts the branch. The cobra lunges, an eye-blink strike, a sputter in your heart. Kwasi and Jomo throw dirt. "Ha-ha," Chege calls, the branch pushed forward. The snake doesn't budge.

Chege pulls back. The cobra lowers its head, its hood deflating. The fire's scent drifts over you. A drop of the snake's venom would kill you, a swift and horrible death, yet you feel sympathy for the cobra. The creature driven by blind desire, by the promise of warmth in the cold night.

"He is scared," Chege says. "Scared and stubborn." He motions for you and the others to join him. He begins to march in place, his boots falling heavily. "Stomp with me. Hard." You march, a rhythm ragged at first then unified, your tempo building. A brown haze rises, a dust you inhale. A scent of history and ages.

Jomo, still on his hands and knees, calls out. He scampers to the van's other side. You join him in time to witness the snake's escape. The dirt ripples, a disappearance into the brush.

Chege hacks the branch with the machete and tosses the whittled pieces into the fire. "Let us keep our eyes open today. Both near and far."

You sit near the fire. Kwasi opens a tin and offers hunks of stale cake. There are figs, and Chege brews a pot of strong coffee. You cradle the tin cup. The metal warms your palms, steam rising to your face. Ichiko and Minoru perform a series of stretches, a tranquil, synchronized routine that fascinates Jomo. Annabella takes an extra slice of cake for her mother who has yet to exit their tent. Kwasi fills the day's canteens.

Chege outlines your itinerary. You will climb the ridge after breakfast. There will be lunch, and by mid-afternoon, you'll make the journey back to the village. You'll sleep at the mission and return to the city the next day. Chege studies the sky. "There is something you'll want to see." He stands. "Come with me, if you'd like."

You gather your cameras and binoculars and canteens. Chege leads the way, an angled stride you try to emulate. Keep your gaze down, thinking of the cobra and all the other cold-blooded creatures waiting for the day's heat.

Near the top, you pause. Warmer here, the elevation lifting you from the cold pocket that has settled over the camp. Below, Jomo rubs handfuls of dirt over the breakfast dishes. Kwasi sips the last of his coffee. Canteen in hand, Annabella pulls back the tent flap and returns to her mother.

You slip with your next step, the dirt giving way beneath your boot, a dry cascade. Your knee strikes the ground. The binoculars around your neck slap your chest. You attempt to right yourself but slip again. You think of all the times you struggled to your feet, your body bruised, the ice cold and slick, your father silently watching.

Tom grasps your elbow and accepts your weight. You stand and consider his smile, the backing of the wide, African sky. Another step, and while you have yet to reach the crest, the sun now touches your face, warm, blinding. The umbrellas wait, their fringe waving in the breeze. Together, you and Tom reach the top.

The valley opens before you. The lake's shores stir with the millings of zebras and wildebeests. On the water, the geese blot out the blue. The birds raise and lower their necks, wings flapping. A honk, then others. The call builds.

Chege smiles. "Watch."

The honking lifts into a caterwauling riot. The first geese flap into the air, then the others nearby, more. The movement reminds you of a thread pulled from a tapestry. An unraveling. The earth falling into the sky. A journey rejoined, an obeying of instinct and blood.

Close your eyes. The vibrations flood through you. Cameras click, but you keep your eyes shut. In your darkness, you see not the valley but the lake on a faded map, Chege's hands cupped around a spot of blue, a vessel damaged yet knowing.

CURTIS SMITH's stories and essays have appeared in over seventy-five literary journals. His work has been cited by *The Best American Short Stories, The Best American Mystery Stories,* and *The Best American Spiritual Writing.* He is the author of the novels *An Unadorned Life, Sound and Noise,* and *Truth or Something Like It.* His story collections include *In the Jukebox Light, The Species Crown,* and *Bad Monkey.* His most recent book is the essay collection *Witness.* His next novel, *Lovepain,* will be released in 2015. You can read more of his work at www.curtisjsmith.com.

Born in Chicago, cover artist SUZANNE STRYK currently lives in the Blue Ridge Mountains of southwest Virginia. She has shown her conceptual nature paintings in solo exhibits throughout the United States, including the Morris Museum of Art (GA), the United States Botanic Garden (D.C.), The Eleanor B. Wilson Museum (VA) and Gallery 180,

The Illinois Institute of Art in Chicago. In 2005 a mid-career survey of the artist's work, "Second Nature: The Art of Suzanne Stryk," was organized by the William King Museum, an affiliate of the Virginia Museum of Fine Arts.

Her images have appeared in numerous publications, with full portfolios in *Shenandoah, Ecotone,* and *Orion.* Collections including her paintings are the Smithsonian (D.C.), The David Brower Center (Berkeley, CA), The National Academy of Sciences (D.C.), and the Taubman Museum of Art (Roanoke, VA). Her series of drawings, *Genomes and Daily Observations,* appears in the Viewing Program at The Drawing Center (New York, NY). She is the recipient of a 2007 George Sugarman Foundation grant and a 2010-11 Virginia Commission for the Arts Individual Artist Fellowship for her project, "Notes on the State of Virginia."

To learn more about Suzanne, please visit www.suzannestryk.com.

CPSIA information can be obtained
at www.ICGtesting.com
Printed in the USA
BVHW031107070820
585651BV00002B/114